GLENDALE, NY
STORIES

CRAIG SCHWAB

SCHWABOOKS ©

Other Books by Craig Schwab

Novel

Something in the Neighborhood of Real

Plays

Bench Plays

Vanishing World

Theatrecentrics

Theatrecentrics II

Essays

Osmosis

Origins

Short Stories and Poems

Tales from the Red Couch

In the Forest by the Light of Day

The Sky and the Trees

Glendale, NYC

Biography

On Both Sides of the Fence (with Tony Lombardo)

The Lions Share (with Tom Huber)

Jack Kerouac / Henry Miller (with Robert Ruggieri)

Text Book

An Actors Alphabet (with Kevin Schwab)

ALL BOOKS AVAILABLE VIA AMAZON.COM

V1.0

Cover Painting: Thomas J. Huber
"Bob's Diner – watercolors 2010"

**Dedicated to my neighbors
and Bertha Larkin**

CONTENTS

FOREWORD

*You must try to forget all you have learned,' said the old man.
'You must begin to dream. From this time on you must shut your
ears to the roaring of the voices."*
Sherwood Anderson, Winesburg, Ohio

From one of the best writers of contemporary fiction, Sherwood
Anderson – (1876-1941), the bar was set for many aspiring writers
to attempt to tell stories about their hometowns. In doing so, we
learn much about the everyday occurrences that we share.
Despite the evolution of technology as our greatest means of
communication, it is still stories that we yearn to read to better
understand one another. These stories share my memories and
my point of view after more than 50 years living in my hometown,
Glendale, New York.

From the first days of moving here as a young boy from Brooklyn
in 1962 to my current years now a father of three, married to my
childhood sweetheart and recently a grandfather, my hope is to
share the hometown that I know and cherish. These insights and
stories open the door to how much we are all the same, despite
the differences that may separate us. On the cover is a painting by
my childhood friend Tom Huber. It depicts the Glendale Diner, a
part of my hometown (quoting online websites) since 1949. When
I was a young boy, the diner was called Bob's Diner; I have never
referred to it as anything else. According to everything you hear
and read, living in your childhood neighborhood is an oddity
today. What happens when you stay in the same place your whole
life is that you witness changes that make you both happy and

sad. Things are supposed to happen for the better; but many times we lose sight of what others may see as improvements.

I spent my childhood living in a small 2nd floor apartment on Myrtle Avenue. The view outside my bedroom window was Forest Park in what is often called upper Glendale. During my years there, I saw no changes to the landscape. The people got older, like me, and the world lost its innocence. These stories share the beauty and tragedy of growing old and the wonder of a time we all long to remember. If you are new to the neighborhood, my hope is that these stories give you a better understanding of what it meant, and what it means, to live here. If, like me, you have lived here your entire life, maybe you will recognize something of yourself in the stories.

This book is dedicated to you as my fellow neighbors. It is also dedicated to my mother in law, who at 96 years of age has seen more changes than I am capable of imagining. She has moments of such clarity about her youth that it makes me wish for simpler times. Her youth had a wisdom that all of our modern day technology seems to lack. Where we all rely upon all too many sources to stay informed today, she reminds me when she speaks, "All we had was each other."

The stories in this book are about no particular people. Then again, maybe they are about all of us.

Craig Schwab

CORINNA
7:30 AM

The classical music station celebrates the music of Bach every day at the same time. There are no exceptions to this daily slice of classical bliss. Despite the changes in everyone's life, Bach arrives with his progressive chord changes and musical commentary.

Corinna Marshall waited every day for the same time to arrive. She managed to have her coffee brewed and her toast buttered to her liking each morning without change for over 30 years. The years passed in ways she could have never planned. Life is a cycle of blessings worthy of royal families elsewhere.

In keeping with her penchant for tradition, she watched the daily rituals of neighbors who she came to consider her private best show on earth. The voice of the deejay informed her of the time every ten minutes, or in between music that represented the last evidence of reverence in her life.
For years she had attended 8am Mass at the local church. She sat in the same middle row with her head bowed, listening to the priest give his daily sermon. Sermons she came to realize had reminders of what she already knew. Sermons she came to label as too long-winded.
"He's preaching to the choir at that hour of the morning." she would tell the small group of people who along with her showed up each day for Mass.

"We're a dying breed." Abe Jackson said every day without fail.

"You've been dying for twenty long years Abe!" Corinna would say as they exited the church, looking around the street for Sam Matters. He was the neighborhood reporter; he had information on everyone and everything. Sure enough, he would turn the corner and begin his litany of everything that had happened since the last time they had seen him.

With the small audience of church attendees as his loyal subjects, Sam would share his latest stories.
   "Last night at 8:15pm a car filled with noisy *whosie-whatters* parked on the corner of 80th street playing that God awful clatter they call music these days. It did not take long for the police to come to show them a thing or two. Well don't you know at the exact same time, two fools up in the park were carrying on about the loot they robbed from parked cars along the avenue.

   Turns out the *whosie whatters* being there gave the police a heads-up they would have never had. So into the park they go and a chase ensues. They go past the giant swings and through the tunnel in to the golf course. Round about that time, Bob Simmons was walking his dog Killian, the German Shepard with the blue eyes. Don't you know those looters run smack into Killian when they get to the other side of the tunnel. They end up trapped in the tunnel with all their loot and the police end up thanking Bob and Killian like they were regular heroes."

The assembled audience always found everything Sam said the best news report they could hope to hear. After showing their allegiance to the Sam report, they each made their way to the stores on Myrtle Avenue where they purchased their morning supplies. Buttered rolls and the Daily News were the standard purchases, as they all wished one another a good day and went their separate ways home. Once at home, Corinna Marshall made herself a second cup of coffee and spread the newspaper on the kitchen table. She calmly spoke to her cat, sharing the news she read. The cat, Junior, sat on the table listening more attentively than most humans she knew.

"This paper has lost its editor, Junior. Words are misspelled or they disappear at the end of sentences. Not that a lot of this news is newsworthy. These celebrities today have no idea what it means to be in the public eye. They all lack dignity, not to mention integrity. In my day we'd call them hooligans with silver spoons in their mouths. Damn stepped in it is what James would say. James always represented dignity, and if you looked up the word integrity in the dictionary there should be a picture of him."

Junior tilted his head whenever Corinna mentioned James, her husband who died years ago. She had a respect for her dead husband not equaled by another living person. At times like this, early in the morning with stories not worthy of the news on every page, Corinna's thoughts could go one way or another. One way caused her to reminisce in grand fashion about how things were better in the days of her youth. She would tell tales of local dance parties at the church.

"Long before people needed to keep track of each other with these things they carry like handcuffs on a criminal. Long before everyone she knew looked at her like they stared at clocks. "I don't know which ones can't wait for me to go and which ones are afraid of losing me. Not that it makes any difference, I will end up gone either which way. These stories in the paper always remind me of how much better it was years ago. Of course we had less to call our own, but it was all we needed. We were closer then, with the good sense to know where we needed to be. These fools today always need to be someplace else."

She turned on the television, where she heard the only voices she would hear for the remainder of the day. Talk shows filled the air with people laughing about the oddest things. "I never carried on when cooking the way these people do every day. What's so great about making a salad, anyway?", she would say to the screen. "Why do they act like it was the first time people used lettuce in their lives? These people should learn how to be real."

Her morning nap after all the rushing about she did made her happier than she felt the rest of the day. Sleeping at night became less and less possible, because her mind wandered toward the fear of things she might hear come morning. She thought about the fear of someone not showing up at morning Mass and the Sam Matters news report. She thought about the idea that someone may have lost their way during the night when the world was sleeping.

During that morning nap, after being convinced that everything was the same as it was before, Corinna Marshall slept like a baby. It was not so much that her dreams made things look better when she woke up; it was more about feeling that life still had its pleasures. Like Junior sitting in that way that only he could, on the top of the couch, the first thing she saw when she opened her eyes.

Like the silence she allowed herself to embrace like prayers. Like the arrival of the mail with the possibility that someone had sent her a card or a letter. It was a rare occurrence since the arrival of those gadget things, but when it happened it was like a present on Christmas morning. The last time it happened, Corinna carried the letter with her for days on end. She read it aloud to the group of friends after church. She went so far as to tell the group "That priest should read my letter rather than those stories that no one listens to."

She got quite an earful from Abe Jackson over her letter. "That stuff only means something to you. No one else cares to hear about such nonsense." Corinna knew what was wrong with Abe and his complaining, "You can borrow my letter Abe if you want to. You can pretend someone sent it to you." He sat down for a moment in the park near where the swings once carried him high in to the sky. He opened the letter Corinna let him borrow. He read the words "how are you?" several times before falling asleep smiling on the bench.

MORE

8:30 AM

That was the problem from the beginning. There was always a need for more. When it was about the getting they joined hands in a way that made everything alright. Once they got what they had hoped to get, they were on to something else. The getting to someplace or getting something was their only connection. They were getters and not keepers. Keeping anything was too yesterday for them. Getting things gave them a purpose and a reason for living.

The way she would say the word "more" made people uncomfortable around her. Just sitting in a diner and waiting for another cup of coffee was enough to cause anxiety. Her fingernails would start tapping next to her cup as she looked for the waitress. Someone could be in the middle of sharing a horrible experience and she would be listening with half her body, waiting for more coffee.

That they became a couple at all is extraordinary when you think about it. More people would have bet against them lasting than they could assemble in that castle they call a home. How they met is a story for the ages. The husband who's name I no longer remember had a way that made being social with him inconceivable. He had a knack for standing at parties with his glass waiting to be filled. She would take up residence at parties in the kitchen like an inspector at some affair in the city where the food is consumed like polite birds visiting higher nests.

If pressed I would say her name was Odessa or Clarrisa, maybe Contessa? It was something that was almost Russian but with a nod to the Mediterranean. They both always had perfectly groomed hair and their skin was an olive shade of traveled tan. How they became part of any group of people was mere happenstance. The birth of children causes the most unlikely of friendships sometimes.

Showing up for school functions looked as if they caused Contessa to age in ways that Medusa turned people in to stone. The majestic quality she had was akin to some person of royalty holding out her hand so loyal subjects could kiss her ring. The husband's arrogance was on par with some pop star believing he needed bodyguards in a crowded room.

It must have gnawed at them like cancer to find their son interested in things that did not suit their image. The thought process of most people was that the kid had to be adopted. He was nothing like them. He didn't look like either of his parents and his most illuminating characteristic was his politeness. At gatherings he would be the first kid to say "thank you" or utter the word "please" when asking for anything. His parents would look askance at him sometimes, as if they, too, could not fathom where he came from.

While they always appeared to want more, he seemingly needed less. At times, many suspected that he was born immaculate, like some child Prophet filled with grace.

It must have come as a shock when, in the eighth grade, he was matched with Doria Jinnson. His parents must have visited their therapist for consultations on the art of patience and fortitude. Doria Jinnson was a unique girl who colored her hair different shades of red and orange whenever she had the whim to feel renewed.

At some school functions she wore clothes that prompted people to say things like, "where's my sunglasses?" The pairing of Doria Jinnson and Contessa's son Maximus was quite an exhibit.

No one in the class wanted to be seen with Doria; and when you come right down to it, they ended up being the last two kids without a match for the annual graduation party. When Contessa first got wind of the coupling she contacted the school in a tirade about how it would make her family look. The principal, to her credit, advised Contessa that "it's nothing more than a display of unity for the children."

Contessa contacted higher ups who, after being informed of the problem, found her to be more than a tad irrational. When she advised the head master at the local school how much money she and her husband had donated for the new science lab, he approached the principal on Contessa's behalf.

When Doria and Maximus were brought before him, he could not help but notice that they were holding hands. He found the vision of Doria to be humorous but not offensive, and as for Maximus he had a look of being content. He asked them both if they had issues with being put together and they both responded in a way that made him blush with envy. They said, "If not this, then what?"

Contessa was outraged at the decision to leave them together. When forced in to a situation to sit with other parents at meetings, she clearly made her unhappiness known. "My son is being forced to have his reputation ridiculed because no one else has the common decency to label that girl a freak." When she found herself sitting next to Doria's parents during a pageant introducing the graduation class at a fund raiser, she was flabbergasted.

Mrs. Jinnson wore sneakers and jeans, and her husband (as she told her husband later), "looks like a lumberjack who's lost in a forest." The Jinnson's paid very little attention to gossip and to the ways of others. Jenny Jinnson was a nurse at the local hospital. Her husband, in keeping with his appearance, did indeed work as a parks ranger supervising the daily planting of trees.

As the graduation day neared, Contessa was suffering from stomach pains that caused her to miss events leading up to the big day. The stomach pains had become increasingly bothersome, and visits to her doctor became necessary. During one such visit he told her she needed to go for tests. She was annoyed that anyone who looked as healthy as she thought herself to be should need tests.

When the diagnosis came back from the hospital the doctor advised Contessa she would need to go for removal of a tumor in her abdomen. She was outraged, and looking for a more professional diagnosis, went for a second and third opinion. All the tests came back advising that she consider getting the tumor removed as quickly as possible.

On graduation day, Contessa was in the hospital getting her tumor removed. Her husband attended the graduation looking more concerned than he had ever looked before. Maximus and Doria walked down the aisle holding hands, much to the amazement of all assembled. Doria wore ostrich feathers in her red and orange shoulder length hair. To compliment her appearance, Maximus wore a yellow tuxedo with red puma sneakers. Despite being the most bizarre couple at the graduation, everyone wanted their picture taken with them.

On the morning after the graduation, pictures of Doria and Maximus appeared on the front page of the local newspaper. Mrs. Jinnson, on her way to work, picked up a few copies and brought them to the hospital where she worked. After getting the day's assignment, she walked into each of her patient's rooms and showed off the picture of her daughter and her beau on their graduation day. When she walked in to the room and saw Contessa lying in the bed, she knew that her day was going to be a challenge.

Contessa's first words to her were, "I need more morphine!" Nurse Jinnson responded in the way she would for any other patient, "Contessa my dear, you'll be fine. Your chart says they got everything out and you will be up and out of here in no time."

"Don't patronize me nurse, I need more care than normal people."

"All the abnormal ones do darling."

"Did you just insinuate I am abnormal?"

"Oh nothing of the sort Contessa, your son is a handsome boy."

"What does this have to do with my son?"

Nurse Jinnson pulled out a copy of the newspaper and showed it to Contessa. She fell back on her pillow, requesting more morphine immediately.

"Doctor's orders Contessa, you can't always get what you want."

I demand to speak with the head of this hospital or I'll sue!" "There's a song for this my darling, "but if you try sometimes you'll get what you need."

"My son is trying to kill me!"

"I do believe he's trying to survive despite you."

Contessa reached for her cell phone, dropping it on the floor. "Get that for me can't you see I'm helpless!"

"No truer words have ever left your mouth."

Contessa began yelling for help. When two other nurses arrived they looked at Nurse Jinnson and back at Contessa. They left without saying a word.

"I am going to see that you get fired!"

"Oh Contessa darling, I do believe that you amuse me."

"I need more attention than these other people!"

"Yes my dear, we can see that. You need more help than anyone else."

"When I leave here I am going to have this institution closed!"

"And after they saved your life? How very special of you!"

"Wait till my husband gets here! He's going to tell you a thing or two!"

"Your husband is a lovely man Contessa. He looked very proud last night when my Doria danced with Maximus after they were named King and Queen of the Prom."

"Wait a minute? What did you say?"

"I have pictures on my phone if you want to see them?"

Contessa adjusted herself in her bed. "I'll need more time before I can see something as outrageous as that."

"Whenever you're ready dear. Did I mention your son is going to the same high school as my Doria."

"More morphine now!"

JOSE
9:00 AM

Jose Ramierez was a mountain climber. In his home country he spent his days preparing for groups of mostly Americanos who paid a hefty sum to climb mountains. Since he was a young boy, he and his father Juan would take long walks into the woods and up the side of the same mountain.

When Jose was just a young teenager his Papa told him, "We can make money doing what we love." Jose had never heard of anyone capable of doing such a thing. When he heard his father telling him this news, it was a revelation. Qué clase de milagro puede hacernos tan felices? Jose asked his father as they sat in the woods staring up at the mountain. The words echoed in his head awaiting his father's response - What kind of miracle can make us so happy? His father, without hesitating, informed him, "La gente necesita para escapar de sus propios mundos." The words translated in his mind, People need to escape from their own worlds. He was fascinated with his father's wisdom.

The idea of getting paid to show people things right in his own backyard was a moment of absolute happiness for Jose. His father advertised in the local paper, asking his son to help in making his idea more appealing to tourists:

Find Your Own Bliss
Come and See Our World.
$50.00 per person
All Ages Welcome.
See The World In A New Way.
Climb At Your Own Pace.

Next to the ad was a picture of the mountain. On the mountain was a picture of Jose and his father walking on a path. They had Jose's mother take the photo and it captured a moment which made them all fill with pride.

Less than a week after the ad appeared in the paper they got more calls than they could have imagined. "El Gringos amor adventura!" Indeed it was so that people loved adventure. Soon Jose and his father had four touring groups that ascended the mountain each day. Jose and his father climbed the mountain so many times each month; they knew everything about where everything was every step of the way. The business of showing people the Mountain View and the local history was a major success. Jose could not believe how right his father had been about making money doing what they both loved.

After the first year, Jose was thrilled with the way everything had turned out. During one morning climb, Jose was enamored of a beautiful woman who asked more questions than he could answer. He became breathless trying to inform this most curious young woman. She wanted to know everything he had learned since climbing the mountain.

As they spoke, he became more and more interested in her. He looked at her as she climbed in front of him up the steepest part of the mountain. He looked at her tanned legs pulsating in sweat as they climbed through what Jose and his father called "the hardest part."

During every climb it was the one place where it was important to tell the tourists to be careful. He was speechless watching her climb in front of him.

It was very rare to have only one customer, and on that day he could not have been happier. His father had told him "Sus sueños se han realizado," as the young beautiful woman got out of her car. He looked at his father, who was smiling in a way he had never seen him smile before. Thinking about what his father had said, "Your dreams have come true," he watched her climbing in front of him; and he began to feel weak in his mind and strong in his loins.

He forced himself to apologize for not being right behind her as she struggled a bit through the rocky terrain. She turned and sat for a moment holding her ankle. She told him, "I think I twisted it." He climbed quickly to where she sat and knew exactly what to do. Lifting her tanned leg onto his lap, he could not help but express his concern. He carefully removed her boot and instinctively began massaging her ankle.

He took off her sock and slowly ran his rough hands over the swollen part of her foot. She put her arm around him to balance herself on the rocks. He assured her it was only a slight sprain. He reached into his knapsack and removed a tube of lotion which he put on his hands and pressed in to the reddish portion of her ankle. Within minutes she was resting upon him in a way he had never experienced, and he realized that he had never been this close to a woman.

He reached into his knapsack and offered her a towel, which she used to wipe her head and face. He started to feel weak again as she moved closer with every touch as he tried to make her comfortable.

Once she was feeling stronger, she slid her leg from his lap and allowed him to put the sock back on her foot. He fitted her boot back on with the most tenderness he ever thought himself capable. His finger tucked in to the boot and he imagined for a moment it was the last time he would feel such closeness to her. He helped her stand and insisted they make their way back to the bottom of the mountain. She looked at him in a way that made him weaker still, "I paid to see the top of the mountain." He was so taken by her perseverance that he wanted to kiss her.

They made their way to the top despite her mentioning several times how the ankle felt sore. Once on top of the mountain, he saw her face light up as she saw what he and his father had seen a thousand times before. She let out a small gasp as she saw the view, and Jose knew that she was seeing the world in a whole new way.

They stood on top of the mountain, looking every which way possible at the surrounding countryside: the valleys below, the passing clouds and the setting sun. Jose knew he had overstepped his bounds; he thought of the one rule his father had told him every day, "Esté de vuelta antes de la puesta del sol." The words echoed in his head, "Be back before sundown."

Jose had committed the cardinal sin of mountain climbing. He had stayed too long in paradise. He informed her in a voice shaking with concern that they had waited too long to make it safely back. Instead of acting worried, she laughed out loud, advising him, "I have nowhere else to be."

He told her it would get cold once night fell. Again she laughed out loud and in a voice that was making his head spin, she said, "I like hugs."

On the mountain that night, Jose became a man. As they made their way back in the morning, there was no longer a hesitant step in his body; it was as if he could leap into the air and know he could fly. As they both exited the forest that led to the small house where he and his family lived, he saw in his father's eyes concern quickly erased by joy. His father and mother looked at him and noticed the way she reached for his hand and they both knew that everything had changed.

It was not long after that Jose made plans to leave his home. The young girl had something that no view could match. It was something not even money could equal. As he prepared for his journey away from home for the first time, he felt saddened only by how much he would miss his family.

He had his parents blessing and he had found happiness. The travel to her world was filled with firsts for him: the first time he soared above the clouds in a plane, like the birds he saw thousands of times flying in the forest.

The first time he was away from home for longer than a single day. The first time he looked in awe at the New York skyline he had only seen in photos and movies. The first time he stepped foot anywhere besides his homeland.

They took a taxi to her neighborhood, which was as she had promised; filled with so many visions he had never imagined. There were buildings as tall as mountains in the distance and cars going every which way at the same time. Meeting her family was stressful at first, knowing that they questioned their daughter's sanity for falling in love in a foreign country. He could sense her parents' reservations as she made a fuss about being in love. He knew that in their minds, although it was obvious they were pleased their daughter was happy; love to them came with a price.

They settled in a small basement apartment off 77th Avenue. She found a job at a local mall selling housewares. He struggled to fit in, at first not knowing what to pursue to make ends meet. As much as he thought he understood the language, he found himself afraid to speak in the company of strangers. Her friends were skeptical, feeling that she may have acted out of passion, and seeing this on their faces made it difficult to embrace pure happiness.

Her friends acted in ways that made it hard to understand them. He wondered if they were truly happy or pretending to be that way so as to avoid sharing their worries and concerns. He found a job with a local company who did roofing. When he went for the interview the first thing the owner of the company asked him, "Are you afraid of heights?" He laughed at the question and told the man about his father's dream back home.

He told the man about the mountain. He was shy when he explained why he had come to America. He mentioned the cardinal sin of staying too long in paradise.

On his first day of work fixing a roof on Cooper Avenue he climbed the ladder to the top of a house. Once atop the house his breath was taken away by the view. He could see in the distance the tall buildings of Manhattan.

He could see highways and byways with thousands of cars going East out to Long Island. He could make out the small inlets where water rushed in from the ocean in the distance. He could not wait to call his father when he got home. He wanted to tell him he had found a new paradise.

FOREST PARK
10:00 AM

Time passes quietly and we are all but witnesses to its moments. Some moments pass with many people seeing them and a few happen when only a few notice. When younger we take for granted the amount of time we can again and again do things that allow us to be carefree. Once old enough to start looking back, the memories start to make impressions we can choose to forget or cherish for the rest of our lives.

In the late 1960s there were two ways the summer days were spent in Glendale by those young enough to be free of responsibilities of a job. The jobs would eventually come when graduation from high school beckoned decisions that change the direction of lives. This is a story about the years before decisions were necessary. This is a story about one moment in time worthy of mentioning.

Everyone who has lived here can trace their here and now back to one moment when everything changed. One way the boys of summer spent their days was playing ball. The other way was spending time wallowing in the ways that would later place them in need of help. A help many found in the discovery of needing support from a higher power. Some made it, many are still searching and for a few we bow our heads in reverence.

This is a story of one moment that stopped time on a day when the sweltering heat of a summer's day turned boys in to men. For years the same group of ball players arrived at the 81st Street ball field in Forest Park off Myrtle Avenue. There were regulars and stragglers. The regulars managed to spend the major portion of their days playing ball.

They had names like Tommy, Richie, Freddy, Mike, Jimmy, Joe, Charlie, Billy, and Hank. The stragglers were an occasional bunch of kids who showed up to play when they got the notion after waking up they wanted to play ball.

The field itself at Forest Park had a concrete surface. The bases, pitching mound and baselines were painted in yellow on the gray flat ground. On hot summer days under the intense heat the cement became watery turning the solid mass of concrete in to dust bowl. The dimensions of the field itself from right field to left field were nothing like they are today. In the 1980s the field was revamped for girls' softball.

In the 1960s most girls if they bothered to go near the ball field at all were there as curious onlookers. Several girls were distractions for the growing boys suddenly aware there was more to life than three strikes and you're out. Dropped fly balls and missed grounders could easily be traced to someone on the field not paying close attention to a ball hit in to the outfield or infield. It was the undoing of innocence before adult hood shattered the purity of the game.

When playing the field the dimensions of the original park took on an almost surreal quality. For several seasons when playing ball the dimensions took its grip on the boys where the right field fence was a mountain waiting to be conquered. The first few years for many of the kids was learning how to hit a ball off the right field fence just out of reach of the outfielder. When a boy named Hank hit a ball over the right field fence it was a moment of change. The rules needed to be adjusted to allow for keeping the ball in the park.

Hitting the ball over the right field mountain was a monumental feat but soon everyone was doing it. After one season of watching balls land on the Interboro Parkway or lost in the wooded area behind the fence a decision was made. The decision was radical but necessary. Anything hit over right field was an automatic out.

For some kids who would never in their lifetime manage such a feat it was a moment that defined the way they played the game. These kids were the ones who perfected the art of slapping the ball between infielders or taught themselves the better ways of swinging their bats knowing exactly how to have the ball bounce once before reaching an outfielder.

Outfielders were a unique brand of ballplayer in those days. In the manicured fields of today in some neighborhoods with grass lawns cut to perfection, the outfielders of Forest Park would appear to be acrobats in a traveling circus. Because of the dimensions of the field which was like playing inside an alleyway to right field and a long endless tunnel to left the outfielders learned to leap and catch balls off the fences. The ability to time the arc of a hit ball just right turned what looked like sure hits in to circus acts.

Catching the ball in ways that would make any newsreel today, the outfielders of early Forest Park days were clowns with ability to leap and fall on concrete without killing themselves. As the years progressed certain poles on the fence had to be painted white to accommodate for the increasing power many began to display. Anything to the right of the white pole was out.

Balls hit to straightaway center and over the fence were home runs because the distance was considered respectable and uncatchable. As the fence neared the left field wall not a living soul in Glendale could have imagined hitting a ball that far. From home plate to the left field wall was easily 350 feet. There were major league ballparks with less distance. Also the fence itself was like the green monster in Fenway Park. It was designed to make sure the ball would never get hit out of the park in to the dreaded forest beyond.

When playing left field it is necessary to note, it was like playing inside a vacuum. With the sound of traffic on Myrtle Avenue to the right of the fielder and traffic on the Interboro (now the Jackie Robinson) Parkway on the fielders left, all echoes of outside sounds cease to exist. The crack of the bat echoed through the air in such a way as to make every ball appear to be falling like a rocket from out of the sky. The other interesting fact about the design of the park for any left fielder was the sun.

Early in the day the sun was behind the left fielders back as the cars headed East on the parkway out to Long Island. As the day progressed the sun began to make itself known in a most humbling manner. By 6pm it was directly in the eyes of the left fielder as rush hour traffic filled the parkway and streets with homeward bound drivers heading West in to Brooklyn.

It was such a day with the sun setting in the western skies over Brooklyn that the boys of Forest Park Summer's witnessed something they never thought they would live to see. Years later when reminded of the moment, the kid who did it shrugged his shoulders modestly. With Tommy on the mound, Hank at third, Freddy at shortstop and a tied game in the bottom of the ninth inning - Charlie stepped to the plate with two out with a man on third base.

Hank turned to wave at the outfielders letting them know to be ready. Charlie was notorious for bouncing balls off the fences for doubles and triples. There was no nonsense of shifting players from one side of the field to the other to make it harder for a hitter to get a hit. The game had purity and a dignity that made every player equal.

With the sun blaring in to the eyes of the left fielder he tried desperately to shield his eyes with his glove. There were no magical sunglasses that cut down glare and made the field appear in shaded light. At best a player could pull his hat down over his far head in an attempt to block out the sun while squinting his eyes like Clint Eastwood in the Good, the Bad and the Ugly.

Tommy, the pitcher could spin his body like a contortionist making batters step away from the plate because they momentarily had no idea where the ball was headed. He was the team's secret weapon in tight games. Hank at third base was a human vacuum when it came to ground balls. The running joke for years when playing opposing teams from other neighborhoods: "ground balls go to third base to die." He had an arm like a canon.

Richie, the first baseman was the first kid in Glendale to get a batting glove. He didn't use it when he got up to bat. He put it on to soften the sting when Hank threw balls from third base.

The sun in the sky was at its last surrendering peak, burning straight in to the eyes of the left fielder. Tommy threw the ball to Charlie who adjusted himself off the plate glancing momentarily upward and out towards left field. The crack of the bat had a sound that measures the speed of time in a way that makes for perfect moments.

The ball sailed high in alignment with the suns glare in the distant skies over Brooklyn. The left fielder lost it in the sun. Panic took over as he stumbled backwards closer and closer to the fence. Knowing there was no way to catch the ball he stepped away from the fence waiting for it to carom off the top. As if it was happening in slow motion he turned to glance at the runner on third measuring his throw to home. Staring straight up at the blue sky he saw something happen that no one alive in Glendale thought was possible.

The ball did not hit the fence. It did not carom off the fence and bounce back in to his glove. There was no play to be made. The ball cleared the left field fence for the first time in Glendale history. In what could only be described as shock the left fielder turned to check if his eyes were playing tricks on him. Hank standing at third base dropped his glove, took off his baseball cap and rubbed his head. Tommy looked in at Charlie who was still standing at home plate holding his bat.

When Charlie finally dropped the bat and started to trot around the bases we knew he had ushered in a new era of playing ball in Forest Park. As the years went by, fewer and fewer kids played ball. A lot of kids went their separate ways after graduating from school. Some went to places that would change their minds. Others went to places that would change their hearts. A few went to places that challenged their souls. Many left and never came back.

Every so often I walk past the Forest Park ball field. I look at the changed dimensions of the park and smile. Sometimes I hear the voices of the kids I knew back then. I wonder where they went and I hope they are all doing well.

I think about how I felt when that ball went over my head as I played left field that day. When I walk my dog I look around on the ground for the ball Charlie hit. We never found it.

GERTRUDE
11:00AM

Gertrude McKenna has been reading the same book for 15 years. She found it in a hall closet behind the front door when she moved into her house. Before she found the book she visited the library at least once a week. After discovering it wrapped in an old towel she never again needed to read anything else.

The book was a handwritten journal by the man who lived in the apartment before she moved in. It was over 1000 pages long. The leather cover of the book was worn in a way that defined its many days and nights of being held by the man who gave only his first name - Darwin. She had never heard of anyone with such a name. The only time she ever heard the name was when people wanted to discourage her from believing in God.

Gertrude McKenna believed in God because it was the only thing she inherited from her parents that she could not smell or touch. Her faith had been tested many times during her life. She had years when she doubted everything she ever learned. She always came back to the one thing she knew gave her comfort.

In the book, Darwin had written on the first page - "If I can't talk to you who else is there to believe in?" Every day for 40 years Gertrude opened to these words and like she was about to pray, turned to the next page in Darwin's life story. Darwin was born in the same neighborhood where he died. Darwin knew everything there was to know about the place she called home.

Some entries were scrawled in a way that forced her to resort to using a magnifying glass to make out the words. When she had to struggle to make out what Darwin was saying she would talk to the pages as if it were alive - "Jeeze Louise Darwin," she would complain, "You need to stop mumbling and say what is on your mind."

She would laugh at herself for carrying on like she did, but it always made sense to talk to the book like it was a real person. When Darwin grew up he lived in a second floor apartment on Myrtle Avenue. He described the apartment in a most direct manner labeling it as railroad rooms without a way out of town.

Darwin grew up in what he called the best of times and the worst of times. He displayed no embarrassment for channeling other writers who Gertrude knew quite well. On days after she had an urge to leave her apartment and walk the streets Darwin described in vivid detail from his youth, she felt the same excitement he expressed or the severe disappointment he tried to convey in ways that she did not fully understand.

She stood on the corner of 81st Street and Myrtle Avenue near the entrance to Forest Park. She remembered how he described the view from the same place when he was just a boy.

He mentioned the names of stores that lined the street between 80th and 81st where he lived on top of the Italian shoe repair shop and the Chinese laundry. With a fish store on the 80th street side of his apartment that had people lined up around the block on Friday nights.

Further down she noticed Cooks Arts and Crafts which was still there run by the same family. Darwin told tales of his mother working in Cooks bringing home projects she needed to do. She used the projects to help her cope with Darwin's father being very sick. The entire summer before his Dad died when he was 18 years old his mother painted the Last Supper while sitting at the dining room table. Standing on the corner looking up at the apartment where Darwin grew up she could picture his mother slowly passing her time when not at the hospital painting.

Closer to 81st street was Mohawks Cleaners owned by one of Darwin's friends parents. On any day, he wrote in the book, "his mother would be sowing someone's clothes while the father stood at the counter welcoming customers. It was a ritual to pass the cleaners and wave at his friend's parents who knew about his father and his fading health. Next door was the grocery store, Sewalds, run by Heinz who knew where everyone lived and knew what everyone liked to eat. Darwin told tales of one of his first jobs delivering groceries for Heinz -riding a bicycle that he described as being larger than a Buick. On the corner was a pharmacy called Jampols. Darwin worked for a time there stacking shelves and if things got really busy, using the Sewald's bicycle to deliver medications.

Standing on the corner Gertrude started laughing out loud remembering an entry in the book about Darwin delivering Twinkies and Yoo-hoo to an old lady with hypertension. He had mixed up the bags in his basket and delivered her medication to the delicatessen two blocks down on 83rd street.

Luckily the deli owner Louie called Jampol and they straightened it out but not before the woman weighed down with a sugar rush started doing the Watusi in her night dress in front of her house on 82nd street.

She stood looking at the monstrosity of a building where according to Darwin's notes there once stood an aqua blue Mecca. He told tales of the restaurant called Durows where anyone who was everyone had spent some form of family gathering. He described in vivid detail how his father would bring newspapers on Saturday nights after delivering the Daily News on his route. The people assembled in the bar welcomed his father like he was front page news.

Durows had a restaurant with tables lined up in different configurations because it doubled as a catering hall for people's weddings, birthday parties, Bar Mitzvahs, Retirements, reunions and funerals. His mom invited everyone Darwin knew and all his relatives to the dinner after his father died. His uncles made toast that made everyone cheer in memory of his Dad. His oldest friend Billy Moran played piano and people danced until they could not stand celebrating a life that went too soon.

Gertrude on her days of walking always found her way up in to the park. The view was not the same as when Darwin lived there. Instead of a tree and several benches at the top to the right of the ball field, there's now a tribute in stone to the community members lost on 9-11. She stood for a moment reflecting on the names listed. Each person she had a feeling walked the same streets and each one deserved to be remembered in a special way.

She looked at the names with a reverence that made her cry. Darwin's description of the same spot was totally different when he was a young boy. Back then there was a single tree with benches on either side where each morning the old gang would assemble. Darwin wrote in a most excited way about "Bags of jelly donuts, crumb cake and pretzel rolls from the Glendale Bakery across 80th street where we would devour our treats each morning like sacraments from heaven."

Gertrude stood for a moment thinking this spot with the commemorative tribute to fallen neighbors and friends was always sacred ground. She recalled Darwin's words about falling asleep with a girl named Dot on the benches. How he promised his left shoulder would always belong to her after she cried herself to sleep the night her mother died.

Gertrude looked at the swings past the newly designed playground which was nothing more than a huge round circle with spraying fountains during Darwin's youth. The words expressed about those swings made her yearn to sit on one. She lifted her feet and rocked for a moment in motion having almost forgotten how to kick her legs out in front of her and soar higher and higher. She felt herself half afraid of falling and the other side of feeling young again.

For a moment she could see her husband standing at the top of the stairs smiling and waving at her. The thrill of thinking she could fly made her giggle. She stopped pumping her legs and waited for the swing to come to a standstill. Placing her feet back on the ground she started to weep. She thought about her husband and the years they never had together. She thought about asking someone how to add his name to the stone at the top of the stairs. Walking away from the swings she glanced as the sun was slowly fading in the sky behind her. She thought of Darwin describing the time of day when shielding your eyes playing the outfield was impossible.

  She stood on the concrete in what she knew was the same place Darwin stood as a young boy. She stared right in to the sun wishing it was all a dream.

JESS RUBY NOON

Jess Ruby was convinced her neighbors were members of a notorious gang she heard about on television. She watched them from her upstairs sitting room peeking through her homemade curtains that she knew would never tear like the store bought ones she peeked through last summer.

It was the summer her daughter gave her a book entitled Infinite Jest to read. The reviews her daughter read said the writer David Forster Wallace was a genius. They said he was the best writer to come along in America since Ernest Hemingway. Her daughter Margaret Ruby meant well but in giving her such a work of contemporary fiction she nearly caused the heartache that followed.

Not that anyone would blame Margaret or the novel outright, but such things take their toll on an aging mind. It was during the reading of the book that Jess Ruby started hearing voices outside her windows. At first she took it be neighborhood kids doing silly things that she herself witnessed as unacceptable behavior in the modern world.

She saw the police commissioner himself on the nightly news telling the public there would be more leniency for crimes like spitting, drinking in public and use of marijuana. At first she was startled by these announcements and at her age thought it best explained what her own mother always said about bad behavior, "We're all going to hell in a hand basket."

Sitting alone all day in her home she had the oddest thoughts and memories. Sometimes she swore it was night time when it was quite obvious the sun was shining through the blinds. Other times she swore the voices she heard were the 15 cousins and 7 brothers and sisters she shared her home with as a child.

She even took to calling out their names telling them to be quiet - "Daddy and Uncle Ralphie worked all night so hush now!" she would whisper out loud in to the empty rooms.
"What's this world coming to when you can't allow your poor old dad his much needed sleep?"

Which brings the need for sharing this story to its necessary point of view? Jess Ruby was in many ways a lone survivor. Yes there were several others still alive from her life, but many were too old to remember each other and some just stopped caring. Jess Ruby lived her days the same way for so long not much mattered about who was still alive or for that matter who had died. Her daughter long decided to stop telling her things. It was best to let her believe what she wanted to believe and leave well enough alone.

That is until she got it in her mind that her neighbors were plotting things she had heard about on the news. The anchor on the nightly news said "These people are everywhere and will stop at nothing to make themselves known." She mentioned her concerns to her daughter who was in no mood to entertain such notions. "Ma, our neighbors are from Italy. They can't understand what you say because they don't speak English."

"How can they own a house and not speak English?"

"It's the way it is now."

"We had people from Italy living down the block from us when I was growing up. They sent their children to school with my brothers and sisters and before you knew it everyone understood each other."

"They're too old to learn another language."

"Nonsense, no one is ever too old to learn anything."

"Ma, let's eat our dinner and we can talk about it later."

The years had made life difficult for Margaret, who managed to spend her nights after working all day reading and watching her shows. She especially liked to imagine herself on shows like "Survivor" where her smartness for details would outlast others with strengths and cunning ways. She watched these shows with a deep understanding of how the manipulative ways of others always tried to undermine the best people. In her room she plotted ways to escape without ever actually planning to go anywhere.

Jess Ruby in the middle of the night would pace the first floor of the house she lived in checking windows and making certain the locks on the doors were tightly shut. She peeked out her windows when she heard the slightest sound outside. Margaret would hear her while lying in bed trying to sleep and monitor her mother's movements.

It was on that night when Jess Ruby read the last chapter in the biggest book she ever remembered reading that she heard the ruckus on the corner. A man's voice was heard loud and clear asking for an explanation.

A woman's voice responded in a most cautious voice saying - "There's nothing to tell. I was lonely and he asked me to go out with him."

The man's voice replied in a most heart breaking fashion with his words cracking under the strain of his convictions. "But you go out with me?" Jess Ruby stood peeking through the curtains uncertain as to which one she was rooting for most. Margaret came downstairs and scolded her mother for not being in bed.

Jess Ruby told her to hush, "There's a love story happening right outside." Margaret became more annoyed telling her mother she was a busy buddy. "If you lived inside the same rooms all day and night you would listen and yearn for love to win out over the hoodlum neighbors who are plotting to do bad things."

Outside on the street the male voice posed a question in a loud outburst that sounded both desperate and passionate at the same time.

"Him or me! Right now tell me?" he hollered in a way that had to wake all the neighbors. Now Margaret and her mother stood on either side of the front window peeking outside. The girl stood staring at the boy with tears in her eyes not able to respond. Jess Ruby whispered, "She loves him but doesn't want to hurt the feelings of the other guy."

Margaret stood staring and sensed the fear the girl must have been feeling by remaining quiet. Jess Ruby whispered again with her voice cracking from her own heart breaking, "Choose him you fool. If you stand there like that he will never know how much you love him."

Margaret went to her mother and slowly walked her to the couch. She looked at her mother trembling and went for a glass of water. She heard her mother say, "He will always doubt you no matter what happens."

Margaret returned to see her mother again standing at the window - "Ma, please sit down its late and that's none of our business."

Jess Bell turned from the window, straightened herself up and responded, "Love is everybody's business. I taught you that since you were a little girl."

"Yes mother, but not this way."

"There's only one way. We can't dismiss how anyone loves another person or how they love their family, their country or the world we live in. That's the trouble with us now; we try to define things differently, when the first way worked just fine for hundreds of years."

"You got all that out of two people arguing outside?"

"He's telling her he loves her and she can't decide who not to hurt. They may just stay together but tonight was a defining moment he will never forget."

"That sounds rather sad don't you think?"

"Sad perhaps in a way that makes sense only to men. They consider things that can't be broken more fragile."

"Their pride I assume?"

"Yes, that can never be perfectly healed. It festers like an open wound."

"I have to get up early to go to work mom. Please tell me you won't be up all night worrying about strangers."

"It's all I do now my darling, they're the only ones who listen."

WHILE AWAY THE WINTER DEBRIS 1PM

While Away the Winter Debris

The slogan was the brainstorm of Bobby D who along with his brother promised to clear snow from anywhere no matter how many inches fell. Residents quickly contacted Bobby D and his brother Sammy D asking they be added to the growing list of customers. The brothers had no idea how popular the promise of snow removal.

As young boys when it snowed they had the brilliant idea to knock on neighbors doors in a quest for payment doing something they knew everyone hated to do. Bobby D and Sammy D enjoyed shoveling. There was no rhyme or reason for why such a tedious task gave them joy.

They studied weather patterns in their early teens and planned for snow days off from school. When the right amount of snow fell they set out at 6am knowing store owners along Myrtle Avenue would welcome their enthusiastic approach to shoveling sidewalks. Up and down the avenue they would go from establishment to establishment offering their help.

On a snow day in the winter of 1969, the D brothers made a whopping $486.00 shoveling snow. The money was a windfall enabling them to purchase two pairs each of the coveted only sneaker worth talking about from that era in time - Chuck Taylor's Converse.

The reason for two pairs each was in keeping with their expectations to wear them out by summer's end during the upcoming baseball season.

That sneakers would be the catalyst for making them successful businessmen never occurred to them as young boys.

It was in the summer of 1968 they both realized they had to do something or their playing days were over. By August of that year they took to putting newspaper inside the one pair of Converse sneakers their parents could afford. The newspaper by day's end on the hot concrete in Forest Park off 81st street left the soles of their feet blistering and their socks torn. Many of the other kids had new pairs of sneakers every other week.

The elite sneakers that year were by Puma and the Cadillac of that summer Converse All Stars in leather. When Johnny Matz showed up wearing them every kid marveled at the way his feet seemed to glide from base to base like he was flying.

In the summer of 1968, every kid worth their salt knew about sneakers. They were sold in two places on Myrtle Avenue, Gelobters a few blocks past Fresh Pond Road and Joes Army and Navy Store all the way down near Wycoff Avenue. On any given Saturday kids from all the surrounding neighborhoods would be in the two stores buying their dream footwear.

Converse sneakers came in two colors - black and white. The white was an off white cream color that at times took on a yellowish tint when worn for days on end.

The black worn with the right socks made some kids look slower than they actually were which created quite a sensation when playing games like running bases. One kid Mickey Morn had the genius idea to wear black socks with the black Converse sneakers on and although it was a major taboo in appearance he never got caught running bases. The illusion made him look sluggish and no matter how many times the guys played running bases, because of his choice in foot fashion no one took him serious.

It was in that summer of 1968 after a horribly sticky 90 degree day Bobby D and Sammy D sat on the park bench rubbing their aching feet.

"We have to do something about our sneakers Sammy," Bobby told his brother as they peeled off their socks and looked at the bleeding blisters near their big toes. "At this rate by summer's end we will be cripples!" Sammy said trying to ease the pain of his feet by spitting in his hand and rubbing at the wounds.

Both brothers would argue for the remainder of their lives who came up with the idea. Sitting on the bench with the sun fading in the sky, instead of going home they wandered in to the tunnel behind right field. It was a small walking tunnel that separated the ball field from the golf course on the other side of the parkway.

The tunnel served as home base when they played games like ring-a-leaveo. It was a game that was played by upwards of 40 kids with 20 on a side. The object of the game was a massive manhunt. A sort of ultimate hide n seek extravaganza.

One team went out to hide and the other counted to 100 before going to find them. Years later both brothers would laugh at the dimensions agreed upon for the game. The rules were quite simple, run - hide and wait to be caught. Because of the number of kids playing the team that set out in the morning to hide, hid all day. The team made to be the searchers looked all day.

No kid as far as they knew cared very much which side they were on. It became obvious early on the hiders had more fun hiding then the searches had looking for them.

The boundaries were ridiculous when Bobby D and Sammy D remembered years later where they had to go when hiding or searching. From Woodhaven Boulevard and Myrtle Avenue to Fresh Pond Road and Myrtle Avenue and all points north and south this included the Golf Course.

Thinking back the brothers both agreed anyone who ever got caught playing ring-a-leaveo wasn't trying very hard. Standing in the tunnel on that fateful day in the summer of 1968 the D brothers had a revelation. Standing barefoot on the cooler cement inside the tunnel they both looked at a rubber tire that had somehow made its way from the parkway above.

Despite the realization that there really was not anything that made the tire special, the idea of what it meant to them in that instant was on the order of salvation.

"Ain't the soles of our sneakers made of rubber?" one of them said to the other.

"With the right amount of ingenuity we could maybe use that tire?" Responded the other although they never quite could agree who said what or when.

"Where do you get off knowing anything about ingenuity?"

"I have good ideas from time to time. Like how we can figure out a way to melt that rubber tire, dip our sneakers in the rubber and when it dries, new sneakers!"

"That's the most retarded thing I ever heard."

"Yeah and man flies in the sky because it sounded like a dumb idea at the time."

"So you really want to try this idea of yours?"

"What do we got to lose?"

"Except ruining two perfectly good pairs of the only sneakers we own?"

"Perfectly good pairs with holes on the bottom that make our feet bleed."

"We could ask Mom and Dad to get us new ones?"

"And have them freak out about how soon it's been since we needed new sneakers?"

"Ok so how do we try this idea of yours?"

"We need to figure out how to melt a part of that tire?"

"Duh, burning it is the only way I can see."

That fateful day in 1968 changed how the D brothers approached life for the remainder of their lives. Rather than risk the wrath of their parent's anger over not being able to keep pace with the things their kids needed, the D brothers plotted what would become the first of many ideas and schemes together.

On a rather hellish night of high temperatures they left their home across the street on Myrtle Avenue and headed toward the tunnel. Once inside the tunnel they spent an excruciating number of hours trying to ignite the rubber tire with a lighter they managed to steal from their parents. After nearly three hours exhausted and unable to make the appropriate fire inside the tire they both stared at a piece of fallen branch on one side of the tunnel.
They had not noticed it earlier and both agreed years later it was divine intervention that placed that branch on the ground.

They carried the branch to the center of the tunnel and placed the tire on top of it. They lit the branch and watched it ignite in a furious blaze.
They stood back as black smoke emanated from the fire which quickly became so intense they ran from the tunnel choking. They watched the tunnel fill with smoke billowing from both sides. They both instinctively hid near the backstop on the ball field aware the fire could summon fire engines and concerns they both knew would be hard to explain to anyone.

After nearly another hour, no fire engines came with their sirens blaring down Myrtle Avenue or up on the Interboro Parkway. They watched as cars slowly passed the smoking debris and hurried on their way in to Brooklyn and out towards Long Island.

As the smoke slowly disappeared the Brothers D ran to the tunnel looking at the mess inside. They could see the melted rubber from the tire and removed their sneakers in a mad dash to dip them in the magical elixir. They both looked in to one another's eyes not knowing the proper number of seconds that would give their sneakers a new beginning. Uncertain of the time necessary to get the proper mix they lifted the sneakers from the melted rubber, holding them high above they bolted from the tunnel with the soles of their feet covered in soot that turned their socks black.
Sitting on the park bench near first base they watched their sneakers coagulating in a way that turned the soles in to something that looked like bear claws.

After waiting the agreed upon number of minutes they slipped their feet inside the newly designed sneakers. The inside of the sneakers were astoundingly smooth. They lifted their sneakers and noticed the holes on their sneakers were covered in a black residue that was lumpy in some spots but relatively perfect.

When they got up to walk the extra rubber that made their feet look like bear claws caused them to clump in the way they once saw clowns trying to walk at the circus. Sammy D suggested they carve away the excess rubber. Bobby D made his way home clumping his way across Myrtle Avenue.

He immediately noticed Tony Astor, their landlord opening his shoe repair store.

He startled Tony as he neared the shop but managed to explain what he and his brother had done. Rather than being suspicious and upset which was what most adults they knew would be, Tony laughed so loud his voice echoed up in the park. Bobby D waved for his brother to join him and Tony ushered them both inside his store.

Tony spoke in broken English with an Italian accent and his glee of seeing the brothers together in such a way had him laughing at times hysterically. He told them to remove their sneakers and once in the hands of a trained professional the Brothers D watched him craft their oversized melted rubber soles in to a perfect streamlined design.
Back on their feet with their sneakers fully repaired they felt as if they could run forever.

Tony congratulated them for being so creative. He said something in broken English as they were leaving the store; he said "tell your mother hello from me." They heard it as While Away the Winter Debris.

Years later when they both needed to figure out a way to pay their bills they combined the spirit of their making money shoveling snow with the episode of the melting rubber.

Their spirit afforded them a means to stay in the neighborhood they loved. On winter nights they prayed for snow. On summer days they dreamed of melting rubber.

CLAYTON DUPREE
1:30 PM

Clayton Dupree needed groceries. He walked to his car and contemplated the few items he was going to purchase. A neighbor saw him and they had a brief conversation about the weather. The neighbor asked him to pick up a few items. Once in the car he decided to drive to a new store that opened up a mile from his house. Clayton had read the service was excellent and the choice of things to buy was plenty.

The new store was located in a mall that he remembered was once a local bar. The bar had a name he could not recall and for a moment he sat in the parking lot sensing yet another memory was being lost. The occurrences of his lost memories were happening more frequently as he aged and it was a concern he had discussed with his wife and doctors. For several years he had been having clear and precise memories associated with growing up but things associated with his present day issues were becoming harder to understand.

In an all-out effort to combat his fading memory his doctors put him on a new medication. The new drug was guaranteed to address AFM (Adult Fading Memory). He had been on the medicine a month already and his wife was convinced his memory was improving.

Clayton Dupree was not sure if the medicine was helping. When driving through the neighborhood he recognized less and less places. He informed his wife and Doctor about this feeling. His wife told him he was being too sentimental about the way things used to be. His doctor offered to increase the dosage of the medicine.

Sitting in the parking lot he had a clear sense of being in the same spot as a much younger man. He had finished playing softball in a league affiliated with the bar. He and his fellow players on the team were piling out of their cars after losing a championship game.

He could sense the emotion he experienced that day as if it were part of his here and now. The new store was lit up with the brightest lights he had ever seen. The windows of the store advertised they were a state mandated purchasing facility. He had never heard of such a thing and for a moment he thought about leaving and going elsewhere. The sign advising such a thing made him feel violated. He was not sure why he felt this way but it bothered him for reasons he was unable to comprehend.

His doctor had warned him about side effects from the AFM medicine and he chalked up his intuition as something related to that. His doctor told him about seeing things and thinking things from his past becoming problems. When he asked why or how good memories could be bad for you was a problem; his doctor told him reflecting backwards might be dangerous to his wellbeing.

In the parking lot he could sense memories from his past and he tried to eliminate the feeling before he got too melancholy. His wife had told him he was talking to her more about his past than his future. He did not consider this to be a bad sign since the future looked bleak. When they discussed the basis for her concern they argued. She claimed to have a better view of the future than he did. Clayton Dupree was not so sure.

He felt good memories equaled better dreams. His doctor told him the latest studies indicated memories related to dreams was daydreaming. He insisted Clayton take another drug which would ward off daydreaming. The daydreaming drug was introduced to the marketplace after a nationwide study showed men over 60 years of age labeled the world a better place when they were growing up. The government declared such thoughts to be aversive behavior. Clayton sat in his car convinced he was having an episode of melancholia.

The worse thing in the world his doctor had told him was to live in the past. Clayton did not think his memories were bad for him but more and more he was noticing people his age only talked about the weather. The number one watched show in America was the Weather Channel. When he was out with friends he noticed they discussed weather patterns around the world the way they once discussed batting averages. If he tried to change the subject to anything else his friends would complain. They told him he was not sticking with the plan. When he asked "what plan" his friends became agitated and refused to talk to him.

In the parking lot he could see as clear as day his old buddies getting out of their cars and looking dejected. The loss of a championship game in the bottom of the ninth inning was a difficult pill to swallow. He remembered the inning so vividly he was upset with himself. His wife would be pissed if he told her another story from his childhood. His doctor would put him on the highest grade level medication for such thoughts.

The last thing Clayton wanted was to need daily injections to ward off symptoms of melancholia.

The longer he sat in the car the more he could see the faces of his friends from 50 years ago. In the bottom of the ninth inning after taking the lead in the top of the ninth after his brother hit a three run home run the atmosphere was indescribable. He was standing in left field with two out sensing the celebration was going to be unforgettable.

A base hit to right followed by a walk and suddenly things were tenser they felt they needed to be. He started hollering from left field "Come on! One more out!"

A ball hit to left field sailed over his head and he watched it go past the foul pole. He could feel the sensation in his body which was one of relief. When he turned to face the field the runners were jumping and down as they rounded the bases. The umpire declared the ball was fair. Clayton Dupree ran in from left field tossing his glove and screaming like a madman.

He called the umpire something that day which for years his friends when they were allowed to remember such things said was the worst thing they ever heard. Clayton Dupree called the umpire a punk. His teammates held him back and they watched the other team celebrating at home plate.

In the parking lot of the new grocery store that was once home to the Mikes Tavern Jagermeisters he sat thinking about that fateful day.

Drops of rain started to fall on his windshield. He looked around at people starting to run from their cars in to the store. He thought to himself, "it's raining again, at least my friends will have something to talk about."

AT THE DINER (1) 2:00 PM

Don't get me started! I can tell you the exact date and time I came in here. Some guy named Bob ran the place back in those days. I have never called the place by its new name.

Bob's it was and Bob's it will always be to me. I've been coming in here so long eight Presidents have lived and died with the ninth guy on his way out and the tenth, well God Help Us all.

Do you want to know the exact date and time I came in here? I'm going to tell you whether you care to hear it or not. November 23, 1963 at 4:30am. I see the look on your faces thinking it's impossible to remember a detail like that. Let me tell you something I might be lying, it may have been 4:45am. I was still too young to wear a watch and old enough to understand what happens when things change.

It's not like anything physically changed or the world started spinning in the opposite direction. Nothing like the stuff you see in movies or read in the papers today. And let me tell you I never expected to see that same look on people's faces again. These wisenheimer kids today with their gadgets going 24/7 cannot imagine time standing still. It does and let me tell you when it happens, it ain't pretty. This entire city turns in to one big zombie apocalypse. Everyone can be seen moping around not knowing what to say or do. There's nothing like tragedy to bring people together. When something bad happens suddenly people are united in ways they never thought possible.

All the mumbo-jumbo about who's President and who's not goes right out the window. It's our New York swagger which no one wants to admit is the same damn thing no matter where you come from in the past. That swagger rubs off on you once you move here. If it doesn't well let me tell you something, you don't belong here. The thing is, we are all the same and when all hell breaks loose, we become closer than brothers and sisters. The problem is it's the last thing we need to remind us just how close we should be. That's what you call pure irony.

But, like I was saying the first time I came in here at maybe it was closer to 5am - the place was packed. You ever see a diner packed at five in the morning? Only thing was as packed as it was, you could hear a pin drop. There were a lot of people standing over by the cashier. There was a transistor radio turned up real loud. Everyone at that exact moment in history was tuned in to the same thing.

Remember I told you how tragedy does that? It makes us all human. It erases our heritage and traditions in a heartbeat. Ain't nobody not touched by something that changes the world. It's like watching a disaster movie and you're in that dark movie theater hanging on to the seat of your pants.

That day at precisely maybe 5:15 or so I walked in here with my father. While most people were waking up or maybe they stayed awake all night listening to the news, we were ending our day. My Dad delivered the Daily News and I helped him the day the world changed.

He parked his news truck outside in front of the diner and grabbed a bundle of papers we delivered all over Brooklyn, Queens and the Bronx. Looking back there was not one place we did not drop off that day's paper; all up and down Myrtle Avenue from down on Wyckoff Avenue on out to Hillside Avenue in Richmond Hill to parts of Long Island on Hempstead Turnpike. We drove everywhere all night long and I tossed bundle after bundle off the back of the truck like nothing you ever saw.

Down on Fresh Pond Road a bunch of people were standing around holding candles and women were weeping like they lost their closest relative. In the truck with my Dad at the wheel he taught me about how bad news travels faster than the speed of light. He asked me to help because he knew there was never going to be a better way to teach me how things change people. He said, "This is the worst job in the world tonight. We're bringing bad news that people don't believe until they read about it."

Standing in the front of the diner right past the doorway, for the first time we heard the sound of the news and the tragic words filling up people's ears turning their faces full of fear. It was on that day I learned a valuable lesson about how news may travel at the speed of light but it lands like the speed of sound.

The very first thing my Dad did was holler out into the diner - "Paper here!" A look came over people's faces that sort of woke them up from the daze they were all in after listening to the broadcast on the radio over and over again.

These very same people had come to the diner because they could not watch the images on TV anymore. The thing is TV news never changes. They get images after a tragedy and play them over and over again until you can't look anymore.

People got up and started clambering for the paper with their arms outstretched and yelling, "let me see that?" and shouts of "oh my God" in a burst of energy like they could finally read all about it.

Now let me set a few things right for some of you younger whipper snappers - you can tune in to your media encyclopedia and see the whole thing played out in technicolor. They got theories and conspiracies about that moment in time like something out of the greatest story ever told. Sherlock Holmes himself could not solve this one.

There ain't a marvel super hero ever born who could have saved the world that day.

Yup, let me tell you at exactly 5:30am I stood here in this diner and watched the faces of people and we all looked exactly the same. Not a man, woman or child cared a hoot about what faith they believed in or the color of their skin or what team they loved. Yessiree, tragedy does it every time.

I sat at the counter with my father because there was no place else to sit. We sat looking at the sterling silver coffee makers and the glass case filled with cakes and pies. The waitress with tears in her eyes wiping them clean with her apron asked what we wanted.

Even though I was too young to wear a watch and old enough to understand the world had changed, my Dad said, "Give my boy a cup of coffee and I'll have the same." It was the first time I felt like an adult sitting at that counter with my Dad on a day things spiraled out of control.

I never had coffee before and I needed to watch him put in a spoon of sugar and some milk.

It was the best cup of coffee I ever drank. Sipping that cup of coffee while people sat reading the paper we had brought in with the transistor radio blaring the news in the background I knew things would never be the same again.

Two days later the lasting memory I have about John F. Kennedy being assassinated was watching my mother taking pictures of the TV screen in our living room.

She kept taking photo after photo saying "Someone has to capture this so we don't forget." My father worked delivering the Daily News for a living and my mother was grieving in ways only she understood.

I never wanted to see that look in people's eyes again.
On 9-11 I brought my two sons to this very same place. My oldest son was old enough to be afraid and my youngest looked around at people's faces. We sat at the counter in the same place where I sat way back when. We looked at the sterling silver coffee makers and into the glass case with cakes and pies. The waitress with tears in her eyes wiping them clean on her apron asked us what we wanted. I ordered three cups of coffee.

AT THE
DINER (2)
3:00PM

You ever have a best friend? I'm not talking about the kind of friend you call up on the phone to discuss your latest news. That kind of friend is special but they can never be your best friend. When it comes to things like saying who's best, things get dicey. People have issues with who's best and who's not.

Coffee please, and two eggs over easy?

Are you listening to me? Sorry I didn't mean to come in here and bother your breakfast. It's just that I have not been around many people for a while. My best friend and I got too close to worry about others. He had a way of chasing some people away. I never blamed him; I wish I had his audacity around certain folks.

Yes, with cream or half and half if you got it?

To tell you the truth I don't read the papers anymore. That's not news, it's a bunch of people trying to sell me their ideas and opinions. What's that? Yeah I guess that sums me up perfectly. I'm a curmudgeon who is very selective these days in how I spend my time. My doctor says it will be my saving grace. Then he told me I need to get out more. Damn doctors, I wish they could make up their minds.

I'm not going to get all slobbery about it. My best friend knew me better than anyone. He had a way about him that made me believe everything is going to be alright. Do you want to know something I never told anyone? I'm afraid of people who don't like animals. There's something suspicious about someone who's afraid of anything they don't understand.

Can I have some jelly for my toast?

You're never ready to say goodbye to your best friend. I only wish my doctor could have the same attitude about living and dying. It's not like we have to suffer through the stuff they tell us they can't cure. You know what it is when you come right down to it? A double standard is what it is. I had to choose when to let my best friend go. He ran out of time to be himself. Best friends should never let one another get to the point of not being themselves.

Yes thank you, another cup of coffee will be nice.

I know what you're thinking. That's because you don't understand. Maybe you never had a best friend. Quite frankly, I am sorry to hear that. People are guarded in that way. They're afraid to share things, which is amusing really. Kids have to learn to share at an early age. They learn to let another kid play with their favorite toys. That's a hard lesson to learn no matter how you slice your bread.

Can I have some sweet and low please?

Then we all grow older and sharing how we feel is like pulling teeth. That's sort of why I haven't been around much lately. It gets really boring trying to pull teeth. No, I'm not a dentist. It's a metaphor about trying to get people to be real. Yeah I do that sometimes, I speak in metaphors which makes some people kind of crazy. It's not like I deliberately try to be obscure. It's a habit when you don't spend time around people. Let me tell you something few people know - dogs and cats understand metaphors. They don't beat around the bush or bite their tongues.

They come right on out with what's on their minds.

Now that I think of it, people who don't like dogs are like democrats and republicans. There's no way they will ever see eye to eye. It's like something inside of them can never embrace something they don't like. Here's another thing, these kinds of people can bark up trees like you would never believe.

They can rant about the things they think is right and rave against what they don't like until it sounds like a kennel around here.

Just the check, thank you.

Anyways, I lost my best friend today. I miss him like no one I ever knew. He made me think I knew what I was talking about. Even when I carried on about things and he had no idea what I was talking about. He never got all hot under his collar or threatened to never talk to me again. I like to think I understood him in the best way I could. I held him in my arms until I saw his eyes disappear. He let me be myself. I'll never forget that.

No, I'm ok, I haven't walked home alone in a long time.

SHOPPING
3:30PM

Clayton Dupree stood inside the new shopping mall. Music was emanating from overhead speakers. He felt annoyed how more and more the music reminded him how he was losing touch with the modern world. He got a cart and began going up and down aisles. It occurred to him as he went past products on shelves there was more food in the store than some countries around the world saw in a lifetime. He had no need for such thoughts and he tried to focus on his shopping list.

As his cart filled with groceries he recognized one of his sons friends. They chatted for a moment about baseball and the friend showed him pictures on his phone. The pictures were a commemorative collection of his father's t-shirts.

Clayton Dupree was very proud of the young man for seeing value in such things. For years Clayton's wife had asked him to clean out his closet filled to capacity with t-shirts. Seeing the picture Clayton could sense immediately the reverence being displayed by the son for his father.

They shook hands and Clayton continued shopping. He passed a husband and wife in the frozen foods aisle. They were arguing over what ice cream to buy. The husband was adamant about having Reese peanut butter included in his ice cream. The wife told him his diabetes could not handle the sugar content. They got louder and louder until finally the husband walked away frustrated. In the pet supplies aisle he walked past the cat food. For a brief moment he remembered the two cats he and his wife had to put down a year earlier two months apart.

He thought about the money he was saving not having to buy cat food. Then he thought about the way both cats interacted with the dog. He remembered finding all three lying on the living room couch on top of one another in the middle of the night.

He chuckled to himself thinking any rumors about cats and dogs were highly exaggerated. He put cans of dog food in his cart and turned to the next aisle.

His cart was blindsided by a fast moving woman who was holding a cell phone to her ear and a shopping list in her hand. She looked at him as if he had invaded her space. As he backed away and tried going around her he heard her say into her phone, "I'll call you back!" As he was passing her he heard his name, "Clayton! Is that you?"

He looked at the woman having no idea who she was. He acknowledged he was who she thought he was as she gave him a huge hug. Getting a hug was not something he expected to get while shopping. From a stranger it made matters even a tad more odd. He did not wish to embarrass the woman by asking her who she was, so he let her fill in the memory gap.

She was talking so fast his head was spinning. There was a song on the sound system he felt was making the situation unbearable. As she spoke saying things that made little sense to him he could not help but feel the distortion filtering through his head from the music. He focused on her eyes and suddenly he knew who she was.

She may have gained weight but those eyes he thought, "My God she's still the most beautiful girl in the neighborhood!" Once he could categorize in his mind who she was his ability to understand her became more clear.

She was the one who caused accidents on Myrtle Avenue. Several times when growing up cars veered in to other cars and once on to a sidewalk because they saw her. She had a way of walking that made everything around her become dangerous. It was not her fault she was born this way.

Watching her pass his front door one night he recalled thinking, "She must wake up in liquid form. How else can she fit in to those jeans." It was a line he would think many times when he watched movies his whole life. He would tell anyone willing to listen, "None of these stars today can compare to this girl I knew growing up." Here he was standing in front of her at the end of the pet supplies aisle.

She looked exactly the same as he remembered her more and more. Even her voice which he only heard once in a conversation they had a million years earlier at a party sounded the same. As she filled him about what was happening in her life, he thought about that conversation they had years earlier. She had come over to him after he put on another record. For some reason he took on the role of deejay at parties. He did not drink and he assumed the role because if he was addicted to anything life, it was music.

As she stood in front of him and the sound system in the store became more annoying he tried to focus on her voice. Very few people he thought would understand how sensitive his ears to noise. The music was escalating in intensity and he found himself leaning closer and closer to her lips. He desperately wanted to hear only her voice the way he did years earlier.

The thought of that memory was making him nervous. The way she leaned in close to him by the record player asking if he could play a song she liked. He remembered the way her voice filled his left ear and the sensation of her breath that tickled his face. He remembered how after she asked him to play the song she stood looking in to his eyes. It was the closest he ever was to a girl without kissing her. To make matters more complicated, as he was leaning in to her lips to hear her more clearly he remembered what he did next at that party. He kissed her. He remembered seeing her backing away from him. The way her eyes turned from diamonds in to daggers.

She called him a weirdo and disappeared back in to the crowded basement. He remembered shuffling through the 45rpm single box for the song she wanted to hear. He could remember clearly the sound of the turntable needle setting down on the grooves of the song. It was the last time he saw her when they were young.

Here she was talking to him again and it felt momentarily good. He had not understood a single word she said about anything or anyone.

As she went to pull her cart away she hugged him again and then kissed him. It was weird. He continued his shopping. When he went to cask register he could see her walking down the organic food aisle. She was talking on her phone. Checking out he looked up at the ceiling of the super market. Her song was playing.

DIXON BEING DIXON 4PM

Dixon says there are two kinds of people, "Those that do and those that don't." I asked him do and don't what? He drives me crazy when he says this kind of stuff. Sometimes I think he goes home at night and thinks of things to drive me crazy. Not that this is anything new mind you, he's been like this since we were kids.

Dixon says people either remember or choose to forget. I say, remember or forget what? He gets me every time with this nonsense. He never has a straight answer for anything. He's a pretty smart guy too, but he excels at making these statements that have so many unanswered questions.

I told him he would be a great politician. He gets all bent out of shape when you say things in response to his stuff. Like the time I told him he should run for this community position I saw posted in the paper. "What's wrong with you?" he starts yelling, "I can't be trying to solve problems in the community, there's a whole world out there!" When I said, so why don't you run for something bigger - maybe president?

He doesn't miss a beat, starts going on about not wanting to debate things. He says, there are two kinds of politicians, those who own big houses with locks on their gates and those who live in shacks with no doors. I say, "What's that mean?" He says, "If one of those people started calling me names I would tell them to shut up. But if they went after my family, there's no way I'd be able to stand next to them debating world peace. That would make me a hypocrite."

I told him there are two kinds of candidates, those that are hypocrites and those that are not." This nearly made him blow a gasket or something because his face got all red and he says, "Everyone's a hypocrite if they can't tell the truth!" I yelled right back at him, "Why can't you tell the truth?" He goes, "Because the truth is twisted in a knot and lies are not."

It gets to the point I have to go for long walks after talking to him. Last time we had one of our conversations I walked myself right out of Glendale. I hardly ever leave here so you can imagine what it felt like to find myself off the reservation. I walked straight down Myrtle on to Fresh Pond road and headed up towards Metropolitan Avenue. It's been like forever since I walked that far. I made a turn down one of the streets and soon I was on Woodward Avenue in Ridgewood.

It was not like I was lost or anything. I know these streets because as a kid Dixon and I would do stuff like take walks together. Dixon says, there are two kinds of people, those that walk and those who drive. I have to admit sometimes you can't argue with his logic. Of course I can't leave well enough alone even when he's right and I say something like, "and don't forget those that take the buses and trains." Dixon gets all bent out of shape when I add to his commentary about things.

"No," he hollers, "that would be a different equation like there are two kinds of people, those that take buses and those who take trains." Which only makes matters worse because I say, "a lot of people take the bus to the train, so they use both." We drive each other crazy like that all day long.

So I start walking up Woodward Avenue and I cannot believe my eyes. There on the avenue near Forest Avenue is a book store. It's called the Topos Bookstore. It's a small cafe with bookshelves filled with used books. I call up Dixon and he says, "There are two kinds of people, those that read and those who choose not to." I could not agree with him more and told him I would meet him inside the cafe.

It's smaller than you can imagine with the books lining the walls on both sides when you walk in. The shelves are categorized with fiction on the left and science fiction hidden behind the front wall of poetry books. There are a few tables lined up on the right in front of a huge counter like you find in an old candy store. They sell coffee and tea and water and as I walked in there's was a heated discussion going on about "what kind of people vote today." I got to tell you that that this place was custom made for Dixon.

This one quite beautiful woman was saying, "Every kind of person should vote if they can." This bookish looking guy with old school horn rimmed glasses said, "How can we vote if everyone running doesn't have anything remotely important to say?" This caused a regular free for all as the place got louder and louder. I started browsing in the fiction section and could not believe the quality of the material available. There were authors you don't see these days. Old paperback editions of people like Sherwood Anderson's Winesburg, Ohio and multiple copies of Kerouac's On the Road and Henry Miller's Tropic of Capricorn and Tropic of Cancer and some stuff I never knew he wrote.

The discussion on voting was getting louder and louder and I knew Dixon would arrive any minute and walk in to his own brain. I found a copy of Kurt Vonnegut's Slaughterhouse Five and started reading it like anyone should if they think they understand war and peace. I even browsed through an old paperback copy of Catcher in the Rye by J.D. Salinger looking for the part where Holden Caulfield is all bent out of shape over where the ducks sleep in Central Park.

That part always made me laugh and I kind of forgot I was in this bookstore and let out a loud laugh that sort of made everyone start looking funny at me.

In walks Dixon in the way only he can enter such a place, like he's been there a thousand times and wants to use a bathroom. He sees me standing off to the side and immediately starts saying things like only he can. "There are two kinds of people, those that like Holden Caulfield and those that think he's a jerk." I tell him there's no way I could disagree with him, but I say, "What about the ducks?" This is one of our biggest issues with literature, how something so simple as where do ducks sleep at night is like the old cliché "if a tree falls in the forest does anyone hear it?"

We have been arguing about this issue since we were young boys. Immediately, Dixon goes in to one of his rants how the tree and forest thing is not worthy of further analysis. He does not realize how loud he gets when he is making his points. "If there's no one in the forest when the tree falls then it just fell and no one heard it. But, if it falls and there's someone nearby, of course they hear it but maybe they don't know what it is they heard."

I look around the bookstore and notice Dixon has become the center of attention. My laughing over reading Catcher in the Rye has been eclipsed by Dixon being Dixon. Coming from the back of the store there's a song playing off a small radio. It's an old obscure John Lennon song off the Imagine album. Everyone around the world knows the title track "Imagine." It' is used to commemorate thoughts related to random acts of violence and is sung after natural disasters. Most people can name the song without even liking music. Dixon says anyone who doesn't like music should be helped. He says, "there's two types of people, those that like music and those who choose to ignore it."

I always say, there's music you cannot ignore because it's so annoying. He agrees with me by saying something way out of the ordinary, he says, "Ignorance is bliss."

Both of us sort of wave at the people who only moments before were discussing the dilemma of voting in the modern world. Both Dixon and I are much older than the average aged customer there and I start to think of a way to make an exit. But, Dixon being Dixon has to have something to say. He waits for a moment and then starts in about the John Lennon song "Crippled Inside," that was suddenly louder because it was so quiet.

You hear this song? It's Lennon's comment on human stupidity. It's about all of us and none of us. It's about being so crippled you can't believe what you are hearing or seeing. Some of the customers stared at Dixon like he was some kind of psycho.

Then the beautiful girl spoke up saying, "He was telling us we are all damaged goods." I don't think I ever saw Dixon dumbstruck. I was waiting for his usual contradiction of anything he heard, but this time he just looked at the woman and smiled.

Dixon doesn't ever smile. The last time I saw him smile we were like 12 years old. We walked to the Forest Hills Tennis Stadium for a concert. It seemed like everyone on the planet was there that night to see The Monkees. That is everyone except Dixon that is. He wanted to see the opening act, Jimi Hendrix. When Hendrix came on the stage he went in to one of his signature songs "Purple Haze."

The audience went nuts but not in the way today you might think they did. They started booing and yelling "We want the Monkees!" It was horrible to witness a music legend being disrespected like that. Dixon smiled through the whole performance. The remainder of Hendrix's set of music was muffled by the crowd yelling and a few tossing things at the stage. As he left the stage Hendrix flipped a bird at the audience. Dixon stood smiling like he had seen a God.

He was standing in that used bookstore cafe on Woodward Avenue in Ridgewood with that same look on his goofy face. I went over and poked him a few times and like never before he was silent. That always ready for a comment brain of his was in love. That's the only thing I can say to describe it. He finally turned to me and said in a whisper, "I think she knows where the ducks sleep."

AGAIN
5PM

Sam Prine was in no mood for his neighbors' nonsense. As the weather improved the noise got louder. He needed to enjoy the warmth of Spring and the promise of summer. He told his friend in a phone conversation, "The winters are getting longer and the summers louder." His friend who had gone to extreme measures to escape the same conclusion advised him "Get out while you still can." Sam appreciated his friends advice but knew getting out was not an option. His friend had chosen to leave the neighborhood by moving far away. Most times when the friend contacted Sam they talked about the "old days."

Memories seemed to be the only connection his friend had for growing old in peace. When Sam asked his buddy, "What do you do all day?" His friend responded happily, "I take long walks with my dog. I read books I always promised myself I would get to before I die. I talk to friends on the phone." Sam thought this sounded wonderful and he advised his friend "I can do that too."

"Yes his friend said, but can you enjoy it?"

As the weather improved the neighbors sense of celebration became more pronounced. They played music late in to the evening and held wild parties that included dancing and loud singing. He thought he had never witnessed such a display of constant happiness.

Seeing his neighbors laughing and carrying on made him angry. He called the police several times when the noise became unbearable after midnight. He decided he was going to do something he had been avoiding since his wife passed the year before. His wife was the practical one.

She was the friendly neighbor who seemingly knew who lived where and for how long. Sam did not pay these things any mind. He cared about logical things like which neighbor was most likely to annoy him on a daily basis. He concerned himself with how many cars each house owned. Together he and his wife of 50 years had seen changes to their childhood neighborhood fewer and fewer people could appreciate. Because he grew up and stayed in the same place where he had chosen to live out his life, he embraced an attitude that made him protective of things.

He told his friend on the phone, "You would never recognize the old neighborhood. You were smart to get out when you did." These comments made his friend feel good about himself. They served to give him the peace he enjoyed living inside his own mind.

On a bright sunny morning that came after what Sam considered "the darkest winter" he stepped out his front door to the smell of spring in the air. He had decided he was going to find out if it was just him bothered by the noisy neighbors or if there were others. He had wanted to go door to door knocking and making his inquiry but ended up choosing random houses where he once knew people who lived there.

When he rang the bell two houses down and politely knocked on a window a woman he never saw before answered the door. He asked about the Bronstein's who he knew bought the house around the same time he and his wife moved on to the block. The woman shared what she knew in an accent he struggled to understand.

She told him Mr. Herb Bronstein passed away during the winter and she was the live in caretaker for Betty Bronstein who was in waning health. The Bronstein children and Sam's kids were close growing up on the block. There were fantastic parties that lasted for days celebrating the children's birthdays and graduations from schools through the years.

When the children moved away they had very little in common and what had been daily reminders of similar things faded away. Sam was standing on the Bronstein steps when he realized how some friendships are nothing more than passing acquaintances. He told the caretaker lady to say hello to Betty for him. She closed the door with a smile that made Sam feel sad.

Not to be deterred he continued his mission by knocking on another neighbors door he had spoken to for years when baseball season started. The neighbor was a Mets fan and Sam a lifelong Yankee fan. The banter between them was humorous and at times quite competitive. When the Yankees and Mets played in the World Series against each other back in 2000 Sam raised a Yankee banner from his roof. The neighbor had a Met flag waving day and night with floodlights that lit up the entire block.

The block enjoyed their daily bickering which was nothing more than support of their teams. A woman answered the door he had not seen before at the Met fans house as well. He made his inquiry as to where his friend was and she in turn advised "No speak English." She promptly shut the door in his face.

He stood for a moment wondering if his friend who had moved away was the most intelligent man on earth. After several more attempts at different houses, he was more frustrated than he felt when the noisy neighbors celebrated in to the night before. He entered the park at the end of his block through a small fence opening. He stood for a moment taking in the landscape where he had for years walked his dog after long day at work. He said out loud, "The bastards can't change nature."

Despite everything that had obviously changed along the avenues, roads and boulevard the park held on to its graces. He walked past the Carousel and recognized a song he knew from years earlier. At first he felt it was inappropriate to hear the song emanating from a Carousel. He grew up associating organ music and something called Om Pa music coming from a Merry Go Round. His trip to the Carousel with his family when his children were young was like stepping in to another country.

The organ music and the Om Pa sounds from places like Germany, Italy and Ireland always made the three to five minute ride on the carousel joyful. Standing on the steps leading up to the carousel he heard a song older than himself and while it made him angry not to hear what he considered "traditional" music, the song made him feel joyful. Without realizing, he started to sing-a-long with the song while he walked up the stairs he had taken many times with his wife and children.

At the top of the steps he felt momentarily dizzy and found a bench to sit down. A man approached carrying a bottle of water.

He offered it to Sam and sat down to ask if he was alright. Sam thanked the man for his kindness and shared some memories about the Carousel. The stranger sat listening as the song Sam knew too well came to an end. The stranger had no response to Sam's recollections but nodded in a consoling manner.

As they sat on the bench together a new song filled the air. Sam loved music but had not stayed frequent with the kind of changes he described as noise. As the song intensified in volume Sam felt more emotional than he had allowed himself to be since losing the only woman he ever cherished. The stranger sat next to him and in a most unlikely circumstance; Sam could feel the man whimpering. At first it was an awkward moment for both men and they looked away in separate directions trying to compose themselves.

The lyrics of the song soared to heights Sam could not fathom possible in a modern world hell bent on destroying itself. The woman singing the song had to be some kind of alien. Sam thought to himself he was not hearing anything related to the noise his neighbors played. This was other worldly. This was from a place he did not know existed anymore. He forgot about the whimpering stranger sitting next to him.

When he looked at the carousel revolving with its empty wooden horses going up and down and the chariots with no passengers; he saw his wife waving at him and his children clutching to poles on the horses laughing. It was a vision more real than any memory he had in the past.

He sensed his wife's hands on his providing the comfort he no longer experienced. The song reached its zenith and with its crescendo the memory faded.

Sam turned to look at the stranger who was wiping tears from his eyes. Without saying a word the man patted Sam on his leg and said, "Gets me every time." Sam watched as the man walked away. He thought the man worked at the concession stand but noticed he walked down a back exit ramp toward Woodhaven Boulevard. Sam walked over to a young woman sitting in a telephone-like booth in front of the carousel. He asked her what song just played.

She looked out of a small window in the booth and glanced at her iPod. She pressed a button and asked him, "Did it make you feel happy?" Sam seeing how young the woman in the booth was said, "Happiness can be sad sometimes." She asked if he wanted to hear the song again. He told her only of he could go for a ride.

He paid the fare and walked through the gates leading to the carousel. He wondered if it was a fluke or if the song could take him back again to his happiest memories. He looked around realizing how silly to be the only person on a carousel with the sun setting in the distance over Victory Field. When the carousel began its evolution, as promised the song filled the air around him.

Instantly his wife was sitting in a chariot next to him. His children were laughing as they held on to the horses going up and down. He could sense his wife's hand on his and he knew life was good. When the carousel came to a halt he looked at the young girl in the booth. He waved his hand in a spiral motion. He whispered, "again."

SISTERS
5:30 PM

Elsie Mae Rose was a proud woman. So proud, she took her secrets to the grave. Her sister Ariel Rae Rose shared the same secrets. She died before she could share them. To understand these secrets one needs to tolerate acceptance and embrace forgiveness as a saving grace.

Although both sisters were frequently apart after their youthful ordeal, they were never as close as when they thought about what happened to them. Life is such that truth at times requires learning to forgive.

Elsie and Ariel began their lives as part of a happy family.

In the years before the Great War most children in New York knew the etiquette of struggle without thinking themselves oppressed. The concept of family held on to values that abided by strict disciplines and a strong faith. Some disciplines required a better understanding of what faith truly means.

When their mother died giving birth to another sister, their father made a decision that would haunt the family forever. He decided he could not take care of his children without reaching out for help. Guidance came in the form of their parish priest. The priest suggested he make a decision which children he could afford to keep and which ones needed to be placed elsewhere. The decision to maintain some semblance of unity put both Elsie and Ariel in an orphanage.

At first the father tried visiting them on a weekly basis. Weeks became months and then years followed by forgetfulness. The secrets the sisters shared stem from what happened in the orphanage. Piecing together their story takes patience many abandon with time. The truth is a delicate flower that requires a special kind of faith.

It's been said we learn from our mistakes. When faith is so strong we cannot believe there's anything wrong, sometimes the lessons skip a generation. When the sisters were released from the orphanage they tried reconnecting with their shattered family. Time is a harsh teacher for some and forgiveness and forgetfulness can often become reasons for wanting space.

Ariel was the wild one. Elsie, was the accomplice in all deeds of consequence. Despite their secrets they both found love in all the wrong places. Ariel was no man's fool. She was quick with a snarky remark for anyone who demeaned her or her sister. They both learned to protect one another in ways few could tolerate. It is said discipline is a personal rite of passage. Some inherit the ability to rise above their troubles while others carry the torch of what they learned. Both sisters carried the torch and it shined brightly.

How it shined came out in the ways they were mothers. They loved their children unconditionally but fostered a discipline they learned while in the orphanage. The discipline came out in ways many would label cruel, harsh and without merit. In their hands the children they had learned fear was a devil without compassion. Rituals of punishment learned in the orphanage became daily reminders of how difficult the ways of the world.

Elsie would fight anyone to the death when protecting her two sons. Ariel would subject her children to a different form of expression. Elsie put her two sons to the same test she endured as a child. Ariel tried desperately to escape by moving her four children from one hiding place to another. All the children lived their lives aware of struggles they could not share with each other.

Elsie found her escape in a way most often described as addiction. The bottle became her solace and discipline learned in the orphanage her way out of the hell she never told another living soul. Elsie's deep secret made her sons believe in God. They yearned for forgiveness for sins they never committed. In her defense much must be understood. Elsie only practiced what was taught to her.

When drinking it could be said Elsie harnessed a cruel mistress. It was the same kind of mistress who taught her to never question authority or express herself without approval. That mistress became her nemesis and the devil her sons met when they least expected. The punishments at first were of a sort that many children growing up at that time knew and respected. There was little room for questioning parent's demands or the laws of the church.

Both sons learned to fear before they could accept love had any value. The lessons included rituals of kneeling with their arms extended out in front of them or to their sides. Elsie learned this discipline in the orphanage and it proved to be the precursor to the harder lessons as the boys got older.

When kneeling; she could stare at her sons and tell them how easy they had it. She would emphasize how ignorant they were and how privileged they should feel.

When their arms dropped from the pain of holding them out, she would smack their hands with a leather strap or a wooden ruler. When she had enough of staring at them struggling to maintain the discipline she learned, she would suddenly become a different person. "Come give your mother a kiss!" she would scream and her sons would run to her for the embrace they both deserved.

Ariel had a different method of expressing the lessons learned as a young girl. She moved her children from one place to another without warning. She introduced them to new men in their lives who they were told would be their father. Ariel's children never knew who to call Daddy. Ariel never stayed with the same man long enough for them to get close.

As time progressed the sisters tried desperately to create the illusion of being a happy family. Holidays included huge displays of gifts and tables filled with food. With liquor flowing freely the sisters celebrated until a look of fear came over the children. All the children knew too well the price of celebration.

Quite astonishing is the absence of a father in the children's lives. Ariel's children never knew from one month to the next who would be playing that role. Elsie's two sons saw their father when he wasn't working. He worked nights and slept during the day. The brief amount of time they were together as a family was nothing compared to what they saw in other families.

At night, with their father working, the house belonged to Elsie's demons, Howdy Doody and Mickey Mouse. Once the television was turned off the fear of what might happen mounted. On nights when they went off to bed without incident they thanked their lucky stars. In the middle of the night after Elsie had drowned her sorrows they learned there was two ways things could go. Elsie would either pass out or act out. Watching Elsie pass out was a godsend. When she acted out there was hell to pay. Both sons saved one another countless times. The lessons were not realized until they got older, how when a small child, the values of sacrifice happen in peculiar ways. Love is a suit of armor for children as much as a savior.

Perseverance wins every time when put to the test. Elsie's sons grew up to be stronger than most children. They could endure disappointments without thinking they were being treated harshly. They could sense things in others most people would dismiss. Unlike Elsie they learned from her mistakes.

When Ariel and Elsie were too old to fight their demons, they both embraced the values of their religion. They became the kind of people who help others without asking for anything in return. One can only surmise they both had regrets for how they treated their children. Despite those regrets their children chose to learn from the lessons or live life apart from any reminders of how things were when younger.

In time, the children went their separate ways. Elsie's two sons became parents, married to women they cherished. They both considered being a father an honor. They would learn things about Elsie and Ariel as the years passed they did not need know.

They learned things that seemingly came about because truth has a way of making itself known. They learned about their mother's demons and where they were born. They learned about secrets never shared. They struggled to forgive her. They could never forget.

CATCH
6PM
(FOR FATHER CHRIS)

If you live here long enough you will see him walking down Myrtle Avenue. He starts out walking from Woodhaven Boulevard down to Fresh Pond Road on one side of the avenue and starts making his way back on the other side.

He carries a burlap bag in which he has two baseball gloves and a baseball. Also in the bag is an old transistor radio that he turns on every few blocks to get baseball scores. The neighborhood knows him only by what he does. He's called Catch. On any given night between the ends of March until the end of October he walks carrying his bag looking for someone to play catch with him.

As time has passed less and less people are as openly willing to share in this simple practice of tossing a baseball back and forth. Back in his heyday it used to take Catch nearly three hours to walk from Woodhaven to Fresh Pond Road and back. Today he does it in half the time and it has nothing to do with him being in good shape. Back then there seemed to be someone on every block waiting to play catch.

People today, he says, have less to do and more time to do it which only goes to prove how sad we've become. On his way up Myrtle Avenue he will ask anyone he passes if they want to play catch. Most look at him like he's one of the crazies we have to tolerate from time to time. A few are amused by his spirit for doing something so simple it shares a bond they miss without realizing it was missing.

Catch will gleefully pull two gloves out of his bag, rub the baseball and spend as long as anyone wants tossing the ball back and forth. He says the fluid motion of the ball when thrown back and forth is better than talking. He swears that playing catch with one another makes people feel things they would never experience otherwise.

When women look at him kind of strange he asks them if they know anyone who sows? He tells them the comfort of sowing was once considered a form of meditation. He tells stories about watching his grandmother stitching a pair of pants or darning a pair of socks and she always looked happy. When he asks people who have never played catch before in their lives; he embraces their curiosity with an enthusiasm for doing something new.

When Catch gets to 81st street he rests for a moment inside the park where there's a ball field. He sits on the benches inside one of the dugouts and closes his eyes. When asked what he hears when he closes his eyes his answer is always the same. "I hear yesterday and the sounds of my youth." If he has the chance to play catch with someone on the ball field his face lights up in an angelic way erasing time and turning him in to a young boy.

Out on the avenue again he walks past the store fronts and houses waving to the bus drivers and stopping to pet dogs people are walking. Those who know him think he's one of the wisest people they know. They ask his advice on things and he shares his wisdom. Those who don't know him think he's a simple minded fool.

They judge one another harshly and are most likely never willing to stop and play catch.

When Catch reaches the Glendale Diner he stops in for his cup of coffee and buttered roll. He never deviates from his choice of this meal. Sitting at the counter he shares the stories spent playing catch that day. Sadly most days he sits quietly having found fewer and fewer willing people.

On one recent Saturday afternoon with baseball's Spring Training in full throttle he came upon several people more than willing to play catch. When he got to the diner he was ecstatic with happiness over having had a three way catch near the library block on 73rd place. He was so thrilled to tell the waitresses who look forward to his arrival every day.

"They were waiting for me with their own mitts! That's so rare today to see kids carrying their own gloves. The thing about a three way is the flow of the catch moves in a fluid motion from person to person until it's almost three dimensional and every throw and every catch happens simultaneously. The ball takes on a quality that is almost hypnotic. The only better way to play catch is a four way which enhances the experience of the ball moving from hand to glove in a figure eight dance crossing from one person to the next until everything worrying you disappear. The only thing on your mind is the anticipation of the ball coming to you and tossing it outward to the next person."

Catch gets emotional after having a perfect catching moment. His eyes well up with tears. He thinks about the one time in his life his father joined him and his brother in the park.

They stood around the infield on a night when the sun was slowly setting in the eastern sky tossing the ball to one another. His father told them both to go to the outfield while he stood at home plate. He could throw a baseball a country mile. They both ran as far as he could throw feeling more happy than they would ever again feel in the presence of their father. His father died when he was only 18 years old. He says, "no one ever again threw the ball as far or as high."

When he leaves the diner he crosses the street again making his way toward Fresh Pond road. He crosses over again and stops in to Saint Pancras Church where he says, "it's best to visit a church when there's less people, it's like playing catch-up with God." On this particular Saturday evening Catch entered to find the church empty. He took a seat in one of the pews and thought about how much longer he had to live. He was nearing the same age his father was when he died. Things like that sort of gnawed at him and he knew no one but God knew why. He was aware of how many different ways people these days think about God. He was also aware of how many different versions of God people believed in these days. He sat there wondering about changes he could not control.

A priest visiting from a nearby parish entered the church after serving the 5'o'clock mass. Father Chris was in the process of locking things up. He was tidying the pews and making sure the windows were closed. He noticed Catch sitting there and asked if there was anything he could do. Catch looked at the young priest and asked him if he liked baseball.

Father Chris shared a love of baseball that had Catch believing in God again in the way he once did before growing old and cynical.

Catch asked Father Chris if he wanted to play catch. Half expecting him to be skeptical of tossing a ball around inside a church, Father Chris became joyous and started saying things like - "The ceilings are high enough and as long as we don't break anything let's go for it." Catch took out his gloves, tossing one to Father Chris. They moved far enough apart to get a good feeling in their arms when the ball was released. Without realizing they both separated until they were tossing the balls so high in the air Catch was leaning up against the back pews and Father Chris was on the alter making dives in front of the statutes of saints. They were hollering louder and louder about tossing it higher and higher.

Father Chris yelled, "Ground ball!" and Catch rolled a strike right down the center aisle of the church. Father Chris leaped from alter bent down and catching the ball came up throwing. The ball sailed in a perfect arch almost touching the cathedral ceiling before landing in Catch's glove as he dove headfirst in to the last pew. The echo of their shared laughter filled the church and Father Chris walking to see if Catch was alright got to the pew and found it empty.

Baseball games during the season start around 7pm. Father Chris looked at his watch smiling. He knew Catch had disappeared in the way only he could. Father Chris finished locking up the church. Out on the street he tossed a baseball into the skies over Glendale.

BUDDHA AND THE HIPSTER NATION 7PM

Trevor Preston roams the streets of Glendale in search of something he calls the Holy Grail. He looks in garbage cans and searches dumpsters outside of restaurants and buildings under construction. He shows up at every garage sale, block sale and white elephant sales at churches. He asks if there are two things for sale when he arrives, "Do you have books or vinyl records?" Since these two items are becoming artifacts of a bygone era, his search has in many ways become more difficult.

At a recent White Elephant Sale held in the auditorium / gym of Sacred Heart School on 78th Avenue Trevor Preston arrived knowing exactly where the books and vinyl records were kept. He had been searching for elusive prize for many years and the annual fund raiser for the school maintained the same look and feel for over 50 years.

Once on the stage where the books and records were stored for sale he began his task of looking through every box and on every table. One of the parents assigned to work in this area of the sale asked if she could help him find anything. Thus began the story of Buddha and the Hipster Nation.

His white bearded face became almost stricken with pain as he attempted to describe the items he had been searching for since a young man. The woman became aware of his saddened demeanor and asked if he needed some air.

They walked up a small staircase that led outside near the schoolyard, across from the meadow behind the church. Once outside he stood for a moment shaking his head.

She asked if he needed some water and he thanked her for being kind. To make him more comfortable she started telling him why she volunteered to work amongst the books, CDs and records on the stage. She spoke in a voice that had a hint of reflection; as if she were sharing an intimate detail about herself few would understand.

She smiled as they walked across the street and for a moment sat on the steps besides the rectory building. "I once found a first edition of The Great Gatsby by F. Scott Fitzgerald. I looked through the book thinking someone had seriously made a mistake donating the book for sale at a church fund raiser. I put it aside and could not believe such a prize could be found in such a way. When I paid the dollar it costs at the end of the day I felt embarrassed knowing such a thing was possible. I walked home to my house telling myself, "I own a first edition of The Great Gatsby."

Of course, few would care and several of my friends when I did mention it had an air of humoring me. They were not interested in such things. I never again found anything as rewarding or more appealing."

When she was finished telling Preston Trevor her story his body seemed to relax in such a way as when you know someone is accepting what you say. He reached out and put his hand on hers and they sat for a moment staring at the people selling furniture lined up and down the block outside the school entrance. He got to his feet and slowly walked in to the meadow behind the church. She followed along beside him silently waiting to see if he would tell her why he looked so sad.

"It was something I owned as a young boy and lost. How I lost it is of no consequence. These things happen. Since returning to Glendale I have been looking for it. My years away are not important. I came back here to find what was missing. I have found the people to be kind and often times as lost as me. I hesitate to share my thoughts with most because everyone has their own cross to bear.

Not that I am comparing my burden with anyone; some hardships are more difficult to understand. I could tell you about my happy times, when much younger and joyful in the arms of the only person who ever loved me. When she left me my heart was broken and now I look for the only thing I am convinced has value.

The woman stopped following alongside and plopped herself down on the ground under a tree. She sighed loudly as she hit the ground harder than she wanted and began to laugh out loud at the sudden loss of air in to her lungs. Preston Trevor noticing her momentary dismay sat down next to her asking if she was alright.

The gesture only made her laugh louder as she tried to tell him how nice it felt to be sitting after standing on her feet all day. She liked the way he seemed to be very attentive and thanked him for his concern. She lay down under the tree looking up through the branches asking him to continue his story.

"Of course no one but me would place value on these things. By no means is it as precious as a first edition. Although things considered precious mean something different to whoever values them. My quest is to find the book and the record that spoke to me when I was young.

I realize in today's world that seems almost on par with instant gratification so many take for granted. These two items are one of a kind. I understand that sounds ridiculous. I appreciate the thought of anyone finding anything of which there is only one of them sounds impossible. So is losing the one person you were meant to be with your whole life. If you must know I can never be with her so these two items give me my purpose in life."

The woman sat up staring at him as he looked at the back of the church in a way that made him look like he was praying. She shook off a mild chill that came over as a cool breeze whispered through the meadow. Without hesitation he removed his jacket and handed it to her. She wrapped it around herself thanking him with a smile.

She asked him if he grew up in Glendale. Immediately she could sense an air of trepidation in his face and she added how she did not wish to pry. "No it's ok," he said in a voice that seemed to be filled with sadness. "I'm a lifelong member of these streets. So was she, and together we conquered the world." It was an odd statement and he realize it immediately saying, "This is not how I choose to spend my time."

For the first time he smiled, he turned to her and asked if she ever saw or heard of Buddha and the Hipster Nation."

The question was so strange she nearly broke out in a fit of laughter but she controlled her reaction and told him, "Everyone's heard of Buddha but no I never heard of anything like that." He shook his head wildly agreeing with her. "It's not so much a thing as it is a way of capturing yesterday once more."

She was no longer accepting of his obscure statements and she told him to tell the story without the mystery attached." He seemed to like her abrupt comment and told her she reminded him of the woman he lost.

Walking around the meadow he began to pontificate in a way that made him appear unstable. She looked out on to 84th street where a group of people were standing around a dining room table for sale. She could hear the loud banter between the people who wanted to purchase the table and the lone school volunteer trying to discuss the price. She thought to herself, "For Christ sake, give the table to them for whatever price they want to pay. In another hour it will end up inside a dumpster." She turned again to notice Preston Trevor on his knees looking down in to a grated hole behind the church.

She walked over to him and kneeling down next to him asked if he had dropped anything. "What I dropped I lost years ago and what I am looking for only I will recognize when I find it."

"Listen," she said with her hands on her hips, "this act of yours is becoming tedious. I have to get back to the sale, there's only an hour left."

Back on his feet standing in front of her he tried to express his thoughts without sounding strange. "There's one album by a band named Buddha and the Hipster Nation. It's their debut album with a picture on the cover my oldest friend in the world painted. They had two albums but it's the first one I am looking for in vein.

There's no mention of this record or their second album having ever been made anywhere. I have searched the internet and been through every box of albums put out by people since 1980. The book I am looking for is a handwritten journal entitled "Zen and the Salvation of Vinyl." I realize these are the most bizarre things anyone would spend their life trying to find but it's what they are and it's my story."

She thought about slowly retreating to the safety of the white elephant sale but stood her ground staring at him and shaking her head. She thought for a moment when a revelation came over face. She asked him, "Was the second album entitled "Love Songs of an Oyster?" He nearly fell backwards on to the grating falling down in to a sitting position on a concrete step.

"How did you know that?" Thrilled she was not mistaken she shared the story of owning a copy when she was younger. He leaped to his feet and hugged her.

"No one I ever spoke to in my life heard of the band no less owned a record by them!" She had one more surprise for Preston Trevor, "I still own it. It's at home next to my turntable."

His eyes became teary eyed and he asked if he could see it. "It's not the one you're looking for you know?" He assured her it would do. He told her just knowing someone else had it gave his mission in life a new purpose. He asked her how she found it. She laughed out loud saying, "White Elephants!"

As she crossed back to the sale she passed the couple still bickering over the dining room table. She walked up to them and asked what they were willing to pay.

They told her a price and looking at the other volunteer said, "Help them put it in their car." Preston Trevor stood in the meadow watching her disappear through the side door leading back in to the school auditorium. He danced around for a moment smiling. Standing with his eyes closed and taking soft deep breaths he was one step closer to nirvana.

THE
ELECTION
8:00PM

In a nationwide lottery held to promote the election for the next President of the United States, Glendale, NY was named the site of the final debate. It was announced the candidates from both the Republican and Democratic parties would spar in a nationally televised debate held in Forest Park, Queens at the Seuffert Bandshell. The location was decided upon based on the ability to handle a capacity crowd of residents from the community. All residents were given the tickets free of charge by members of both parties. The curators of the event were chosen in a similar lottery open only to Glendale residents.

A Mr. and Mrs. James Salanopolis won the lottery and they were asked to meet with the candidates before the debate. James and his wife Sally were honored to be chosen and as they took pictures with both candidates they were aware of the immense presence of security and the media. They were given sealed envelopes in which a list of questions they would ask offered insight in to how the debate would take place.

When James Salanopolis asked the news stations sponsoring the event if he could ask a few questions of his own, he was immediately advised, "Stick to the script. This is a nationally televised event and we do not want any surprises." When his wife Sally opened the envelope right before proceedings were to take place she was angered by the lack of substance in the questions.

She pulled her husband aside and they asked if the nights event could be delayed for an hour. At first the news affiliates were against any delays. They had contracted to televise the event at 8pm.

The prime time coverage of the debate was organized down to a cost to sponsors of 2 million dollars for 30 second commercials.

What happened next is what many might consider Glendale folklore. The news stations realizing they could promote the event for an hour picking up revenue they never anticipated agreed to the delay. They quickly planned to air biographical footage of both candidates in their campaigns to become President. Suspicions began to surround the reasons why James and Sally Salanopolis asked for a delay.

Members of the secret service were assigned to watch their every move. James Salanopolis was a member of the Electricians Union. He made one phone call. He called his brother Abraxis Salanopolis telling him what he was being asked to do. His brother showed up at the band shell 15 minutes later with a group of fellow electricians who had all the appropriate credentials to get past security.

They made their way to the band shell stage and under the guise of checking to ensure everything was working properly, installed what many came to call, "the truth machine." After explaining to officials surrounding the stage there was a problem with the electric grid in the area, the electricians under Abraxis placed a metal grating behind each podium. They made different measurements attached to cables and were done in less than half an hour.

Abraxis signaled to his brother giving him thumbs up.

At precisely 8:45pm the news stations covering the debate began promoting what they promised would be the Debate of the Century.

Both James and his wife Sally were escorted through the crowd as cheers and applause mounted for their moment of celebrity. The National Anthem was sung by Adele as a squadron of U.S. Air Force jets flew over the band shell announcing the beginning of the debate.

The anticipation of the nights events were unprecedented in the history of the country. Looking at one another the young married couple chosen to curate the debate smiled for the cameras. The candidates were announced to the crowd and the atmosphere was similar to a Heavyweight Boxing match. Both candidates took their place behind podiums and waved to the adoring crowd.

As James and Sally appeared to be in total agreement with the set list of questions they were supposed to ask they were compelled to realize their plan could make them enemies of the state. James asked the first question and could almost read along word for word what each candidate would say. Sally Salanopolis was growing impatient with the mannerisms of both candidates sensing they had rehearsed their answers so well they knew when to smile for the cameras and when to sneak a swallow of water.

During the first commercial break the news affiliates were thrilled with the way things were going. Make-up artist appeared instantly making the candidates look fresh and presentable.

Men carrying walkie talkies appeared at the desk where James and Sally were sitting telling them how great they were doing.

After the commercial break Sally looked at her scripted questions and posed one of her own. She asked the Democratic candidate if she had ever told a lie.

The candidate looked down at her podium sensing there was no response written for her to read on the prompter. She uttered a few words about being as honest as necessary to lead the country. She then grimaced in a way that made the audience look in horror at her body. Sensing she was being jolted by electricity she tried to step away from the podium. Because of the intensity of the jolt her hands gripping the podium only made her grimace more pronounced.

Sally turned to the candidate for the Republican Party and asked him the same question. Seeing the result of what happened to the other candidate he muddled a few words about only lying when it meant protecting other people. The same kind of grimace came over his face and he tried desperately to step away from his podium without success. When the jolts subsided James Salanopolis announced to the American public he had asked his brother Abraxis to attach an electric grating to a lie detector hidden beneath the stage.

Security rushed the stage but was met immediately by members of the Glendale Electricians and Carpenters Union who blocked their way to the stage.

Several news stations in a panic to pull the plug on the proceedings were met by members of the New York City Police Department who had gotten wind of what was going on. The Police Department surrounded the News trucks in the parking lot and advised anyone inside they would be taken into custody if they touched anything remotely related to shutting things down.

Secret Service agents began to assemble around the parks perimeter using bull horns to dispense the crowd. No one moved as Sally Sanopolis posed her next question to the candidates. Standing now on top of the desk she asked the Democratic candidate, "Have you ever willingly taken money to support any agenda not in keeping with your own beliefs?" The candidate began to shake uncontrollably before answering.

When she did speak, the grimace on her face and the sensation of the electrical jolt caused lights to flicker on lamppost in the park and throughout the neighborhood. Several blocks of houses lost power along Myrtle Avenue and Woodhaven Boulevard. When the same question was asked of the Republican candidate his stammering to answer caused transformers on telephone poles to explode up and down streets as far down as Fresh Pond Road and Jamaica Avenue.

Several agents took out guns and started waving them at James and Sally. They were quickly subdued by a group from the Glendale Watch Group. Both candidates physically exhausted by their ordeal began to cry for mercy.

The Democratic Candidate fell to her knees and for a moment could be seen trying to crawl away from the podium. James yelled at her as she slinked slowly away, "Do you promise to tell the whole truth and nothing but the truth?" Her body nearly lifted off the ground to the extent she appeared to be doing a head stand on top of the podium.

Her hair became filled with static electricity and her arms outstretched in agony caused her to fall back to the stage floor sobbing. Sally sensing the opportunity yelled to the Republican candidate the same question - "Do you solemnly swear to tell the whole truth and nothing but the truth so help you God!" His arms started to shake and his hair took on the appearance of a helicopter about to take flight.

With his hair spinning at a rapid speed no one could imagine possible his body lifted off the ground and for a moment he appeared capable of flying. He became so afraid of his predicament he screamed as loud as he could - "I can only say what I am told to!" The lights on the stage flickered off and on like a strobe light making both candidates look like they were in a movie from the 1920s.

They tried reaching out to one another and their antics proved to be their worst decision yet. James now standing next to his wife yelled to the stage - "Are you both hired by some agency to act the way you do?" The candidates' now holding hands with their bodies lifted like contortionist above their podiums started to emanate a jolt of electricity that seemed to enter them simultaneously as if lightening had come from out of the sky. Unable to respond they fell to the stage floor panting in exhaustion.

James and Sally Salonopolis looked at each other satisfied with their findings. They looked at the stunned crowd and bowed.

There was a silence throughout the park that emulated the same reaction throughout the country. The feeling of everyone in the United States and around the world being shocked at the same time by what they witnessed momentarily made everyone look exactly the same.

Mouths hung open on faces for what felt like an eternity. The only sounds came from the stage where both candidates were weeping and begging for forgiveness. The U.S. Air Force jets that had done a fly by during the National Anthem landed in the Forest Park golf course. Several moments passed before armed soldiers came through the park wearing night vision glasses and flashing weapons that filled the air with beacons of light.

The crowd of Glendale residents sensing they were under attack banded together holding hands they held high above their heads. The soldiers surrounded the parking lot and band shell. The secret service entered cautiously advising no one would be harmed. The Electricians and Carpenters backed away from the stage. The New York City Police surrounding the news trucks stepped away. The agents got to the stage and lifted both candidates in their arms carrying them away to waiting limousines.

As the limos pulled out of the parking lot the soldiers slowly started walking backwards to their waiting jets. As the jets lifted out of the golf course a new silence filled the air. Several people in the crowd began to sigh loudly with relief. James and Sally stepped down from the desk they had stood on.

They closed their eyes and hugged one another. When they opened their eyes a sea of lights greeted them. Everyone in the crowd was holding their cell phones above their heads. The sky was lit up like torches after a favorite song at a concert.

They all knew everything had changed but the song would remain the same. The sound of an ice cream truck could be heard in the distance.

LANCE CASPER
8:30PM

At first she did not welcome his company. His dog, a rather large German Shepard barked at her rather small poodle. The meeting of two dogs can unexpectedly bring about a good or bad experience. It's been said dogs are a good judge of character. Dogs unlike humans can sense fear more easily. Lance Casper and his dog Max were out walking after a long day of rain. The woman who had a day she wanted to forget was in no mood for interruptions. Her intention was to let her dog Sally do her business and go home to a dry and warm house.

Turning the corner of her block she was immediately thrown back several steps when she came face to face with Max and Lance. The first words between Lance Casper and the woman were confrontational. She demanded he hold back his beast. Lance took exception to anyone calling Max a beast and they exchanged words in a most unwelcoming manner. While they discussed loudly the etiquette of walking after hours with their pets; the two dogs calmly sat down next to them and looked at one another.

As the argument heated, Max as was his nature lay down at Lance's feet and began to lick Sally's nose. Sally was not in the least afraid of the large dog and she lifted her head to allow Max to further his investigation of her neck. Lance feeling the dogs were in no way threatened by one another commented to the woman, "I apologize for scaring you, but it looks like our dogs have a different view of the situation." The woman looking down at her dog immediately pulled Sally away saying, "I don't want Sally getting any ideas about being friendly with such a thing."

The comment caused Lance to emphasize her attitude was detrimental to the dog's growth. The woman started walking away when she felt Sally pulling her back closer to Max. The situation became awkward as the two dogs became more playful. Not wishing to be inconvenienced the woman jerked on Sally's leash until it was quite obvious there was something happening between the dogs their owners wanted no part of. While the dogs intermingled Lance and the woman tried stepping away without causing more problems.

The woman looking at Sally who she sensed was in need of attention after being stuck inside all day while she worked tried to make small talk. Asking how old Max was, Lance responded by saying, "He's most likely 12 years old or older." He politely asked how old Sally was and the woman responded by telling him, "She's 6 years old this Christmas. He was a present from my son who thought I needed a companion."

The word "companion" struck Lance Casper as an invitation to say, "It's tough when our children think we need something to keep us company." The woman sensing an inquiry told Lance, "It's not like I don't meet people and I get along nicely when I'm alone." He said, "I know way too much about being alone." For a moment with the two dogs' content to smell one another Lance said, "Pardon me for saying this," he said in a low voice, "someone like you should never feel lonely."

She took his words as an affront at first and sensing her own vulnerability began to jerk Sally away from Max again. Lance Casper introduced himself holding out his free hand to shake hers. She continued jerking Sally's leash until it became obvious her command of the situation was impossible. Reaching out her hand she told Lance Casper her name. She said it in such a way that caused Lance to question his hearing. Not wishing to embarrass her, Lance felt no need to ask her to repeat her name and they stood under the streetlamp as the two dogs continued to mingle. Without knowing why Lance blurted out, "This is as exciting as my day gets!"

The woman not wanting to pry admitted, "Yeah this is very exciting for me too. I can't wait to do it again in the morning." Her sarcasm caused Lance to laugh. She looked at him as he let out a loud hooping laugh that seemingly filled the empty streets with an echo. She commented, "I can't believe we have not run in to one another before, I walk Sally when I get home from work and again at midnight before turning in." Lance said, "I don't usually walk Max this way, he likes to run free in the park."

She looked at Max saying, "You let a dog that big run free in the park?" Lance recognizing her alarm said, "She's a puppy at heart and more playful than anything else." The woman replied, "Sally doesn't get along with anyone so this is quite a moment for her. I suspect my mailman hates her. I come home sometimes and find my mail dropped on the stoop. She most likely barks at anyone who comes close to the front door."

Lance said, "You leave her home alone all day, she's not barking to be anti-social. Most likely she wants company." The woman not wishing to give away more about herself said, "It's not like I have a choice. Sure I would like to spend more time with her but it is not easy."

Lance again blurted something out that made him appear odd but interesting, "I have more time on my hands these days. Max and I know every square mile of this place. I suspect he'd give anything to be left alone without my insisting we go out walking."

Sensing herself becoming impatient she asked, "So you're retired and don't know what to do with yourself? That must be nice?" Lance looked at her and for the first time jerked on Max's leash pulling him away from Sally. Disgruntled, he said, "It's not like I have a choice. I'd rather be doing a million better things than walking around this neighborhood at all hours of the day and night."

She was taken by his sudden loss of charm and began walking away from him as the dogs tried getting closer again. "Stop it Sally!" the woman said pulling hard on her leash. Lance Casper not wishing to prolong the chance meeting started walking toward the middle of the street with Max at his side.

Sally started barking loudly at the departure and the woman picked her up. She stood with her arms embracing Sally until she noticed Lance sit down on a stoop a block away. The woman knew who lived in that house. She was curious as to why Lance chose that house to sit down. She walked toward the home holding Sally in her arms.

When Max noticed her it caused the woman to lose hold of Sally as she leaped free of her arms running full speed at Max and Lance Casper. Realizing the dogs were about to collide Lance Casper stepped off the stoop and caught Sally awkwardly just before she was about to prance on Max's back.

The woman ran up to Lance and immediately reached out to grab Sally from his arms. Sally yelped at the woman and snapped at her. The woman not wanting to create more of the situation demanded Lance give her back. He held Sally out to the woman and the dog pulled away wanting to stay in Lance's arms. "It would appear we have ourselves a bit of a problem," Lance said holding Sally close to his face. "She obviously doesn't want to be pressured in to going home just yet."

The woman was angered by her dogs reaction and stomped her foot to get Sally's attention. "Sally! You come to me now!" Sally nestled her head in to the crook of Lance's neck whimpering. The woman was confused as Max began licking her toes. She backed away trying to assess the situation without having a clue as to why it was happening. Lance said, "I think Sally needs more attention than you thought. Maybe we should sit down and wait until she lets us know what she wants to do."

"I have no time for a dog to let me know what she wants to do!" shouted the woman who stepped farther away until she was standing at the curb. She looked at the house and demanded, "Why did you choose this house to sit down on the stoop? I know the people who own this house and they don't know you."

Lance Casper petted Sally softly while shaking his head. "You can't possibly think you know everything about everyone?"

She was annoyed as Sally continued to make herself comfortable in Lance's arms. "The people who lived here were nice people. They lost their son and moved away. It's been for sale for longer than I care to remember."

"What do you remember?"

"I remember they were proud people who took care of their property in a way that made others envious. They moved away roughly five years ago. I know how long it was because I used to walk Sally past here when I first got her. The husband used to feed her treats and his wife talked about their son."

"What did they say about their son?"

"How he was in the Army and something happened. The wife would get tears in her eyes when she spoke about him."

"Do you know where they moved to?"

"The husband got sick one night and an ambulance took him away. Why am I telling you this? They were neighbors no one knew. They kept to themselves and never bothered anyone."

Lance Casper whispered in to Sally's ears and slowly handed her over to the woman who came closer to get her. Once in the woman's arms Sally looked back at Lance whimpering.

"I have to get her home to eat. I wouldn't stay on this stoop if I were you. Some of the neighbors are most likely already thinking about calling the police. We protect our own around here."

Lance thanked her for the warning. He stood up and began walking toward the avenue. The woman put Sally on the ground and watched Lance moving slowly with Max close by. She noticed how attentive Max was as Lance shuffled in a swaying motion from side to side.

As they got closer to the avenue she watched as Max put his nose in to Lance's path and sat down promptly on the corner waiting for the light to change.

CURTAINS
9:00 PM

The only defense from being discovered is curtains. Some choose blinds, but they can't change with the seasons. With the doors and windows locked there's a feeling of security.

Differences are sometimes so simple only a few can recognize the wrinkles in everyday life. The years pass by, and the events that happen in every home go by un-noticed; or in such a way as to appear inconsequential. People living so close they can hear things happening in another room causes concern or ambivalence.

When Rosie Dupree and her sister Marie first noticed the changes it was too late to make things better. Their parents had somehow gotten to point of no longer recognizing one another. For several years leading up to decisions they both wanted no part of, there were questions they were afraid to ask. Silly things like where their parents had their bank accounts. Stupid things like where their mother hid her jewelry. Awkward things like what kind of medications they both needed.

Rosie and Marie had moved away years earlier. They had no intention of becoming their parent's keeper. They both had lives of their own and dreams for their own future.

When it became apparent things were not going according to plan, Rosie and Marie Dupree needed to confront their own misgivings about life. The events leading up to the realization caused them both more heartache than any relationships they both struggled to maintain.

Rosie was in a relationship with a guy who refused to commit. They had been dating on and off for two decades which Marie reminded Rosie was too long. Because Rosie wanted to do more with life than Marie ever let on, things for a while were tedious between them.

More than once during their years as sisters they only spoke when visiting their parents during holidays. Casual conversation between sisters can be heartbreaking or thought provoking.

Rosie shared details about her life in such a way as to send coded messages to Marie who was in no mood for witnessing her sister wasting her life. Marie was the practical sister. Rosie was the dreamer. When faced with their parents waning health issues they had to face one another more often.

After a midnight call related to their father being rushed to the hospital they discussed what they would have to do if matters got worse. When their mother a week later fell and broke her hip, they knew things would never be the same. They stopped trying to weigh one another's needs and slowly adopted the practice of taking care of their mother and father.

They had other siblings who had managed to escape to different places. Their older brother lived in Ohio where he supposedly was married with children. No one in the family ever visited him and no pictures of his family ever materialized.

Another brother lived in California with his significant other. Their father once commented after receiving a birthday card from the son in California signed, Billy and Ray, "What kind of name is Ray for a girl?" Both Rosie and Marie had no intention of informing their parents how things turned out.

For parents to conform to which one's they can depend upon when older gets comical and complex. Their mother doted on her sons and when dusting around the house would always make certain to clean the pictures of her sons while letting her daughter's photos collect dust. The muted glasses on the frames atop the fireplace were a sure sign of what mattered most to her.

Both Rosie and Marie paid these things little mind through the years because their father doted on them in the same way. When it became obvious their parents were no longer capable of taking care of themselves both Rosie and Marie began seeing more of each other. A year after being turned in to caretakers Rosie announced she had sent her noncommittal boyfriend packing.

She confided to Marie, "I should have trusted your judgement years ago." Marie not wishing to sound like "I told you so," tried comforting her sister saying, "You did the best you could for longer than he deserved." Not wanting to waste money they discussed which one of them had the best apartment. They moved in together in Marie's apartment which was closest to their parent's house. The very first thing they did was decorate the apartment choosing which one had the best taste in furniture.

Rosie had a couch that made binge watching movies more comfortable. Marie had a dining room table that made sharing meals more pleasurable. They had not shared the same space since young girls and soon realized how much they missed one another.

They reached out to their brothers informing them both about their parent's problems. The one in Ohio promised to visit as soon as he could get away from his job. The one in California invited them to stay with him if they were ever out that way. Sensing they were on their own, Rosie and Marie Dupree set about making a schedule as to which one would be on duty to help their mom and dad. Their father stopped recognizing them after he came home from the hospital. He referred to them as "the lovely nurses."

Their mother spent her days dusting and cooking. The pictures of their brothers on the fireplace mantelpiece never looked cleaner. As each episode occurred changing the direction of how things were going Rosie and Marie became even closer. They started to look more alike than they had ever imagined.

They fit in to one another's clothes and when speaking they finished one another's sentences. After several years of maintaining their parents comfort they decided it was time to get information. Asking their mother about bank accounts and private information was like pulling teeth. Their father had no idea what day it was no less where anything was anymore. They made inquiries about what their options would be in the event one or both of their parents needed more care than they were capable of giving.

Trying to open the curtains that their parents guarded for years was complex and tiresome. When both parents were in hospitals at the same time they began to search the house for clues about things they needed to know more about.

In a bedroom closet they discovered a box filled with birthday cards and Father's Day cards they had both given to their Dad through the years. They discovered a collection of letters from their brother Billy in California asking his parents for their blessing so he could feel happy about his life's decisions. Several of the envelopes were never opened. They discovered stock statements declaring their father had invested his money in Apple. When they asked their mother about the stock options, she responded, "Your father likes apples."

His last memory was when he took all of you kids' apple picking in Upstate New York. Who knew he'd invest in something worth anything." Realizing they were going to be taken care of after their parents passed made Rosie and Marie nervous. They never anticipated they would have anything but grief. When the health care bills mounted they had to make plans for selling the Apple stock. When turning over the stocks to a broker who commented, "This is unheard of for anyone to be that smart." They both responded, "Our Dad liked apples."

With the changes came the need for more decisions. It became obvious their parents would never again return to the house they shared as a family. The decision to sell the house or move in to it became a daily issue between them. They argued over whether returning to their parent's home would give the independence they yearned for, or if it would remind them they never got away.

In the end they decided to move in to their childhood home. It had more space than the apartment they shared. It would give them time to weed through their parents belongings. The first thing they both agreed to do was remove the pictures from the fireplace mantel.

They changed the curtains on the front window from a dark shaded blue to white lace. They could not believe how the sun made everything look brighter.

AT THE
DINER(3)
11:00PM

Sitting in the back of the diner the man looked distraught. He kept looking at his phone as if he was willing it to ring. Several people at nearby tables noticed him as he sighed loudly. The waitress kept pouring him fresh cups of coffee. After his fifth cup she asked if he wanted anything else. He looked at her and replied, "Answers."

Instead of walking away she sat down in the booth and said, "What's the question?"

Taking a sip from his cup he looked around noticing he had an audience. He apologized for making a fool of himself and shook his head sadly. A woman from a nearby table said, "It can't be that bad?" He thanked her for the reassurance and whispered "and now she's gone."

"Who's gone?" asked the waitress.

"I think her name was Moxie. She was an elderly lady on my block. I saw her every day taking a walk from her front stoop up one side of the block and back. She always wore the same blue windbreaker and a fishermen's hat on her head.

She waved as she passed my house and I nodded at her. This went on for years. Until one day during the winter last year she was attempting to shovel snow on her sidewalk. I could see she was struggling so I went to offer my assistance. She was very grateful telling me how the snow piled up faster than she could remember. I sprinkled salt on the sidewalk when I was done clearing the snow away and she offered to give me money. I told her it was not necessary and she asked me inside for a cup of tea.

She entered her apartment removing her windbreaker which I knew was no match for the cold outside. I told her she should have a warmer coat if she's going to go outside.

She told me "walking makes me think its warmer." I told her she needed to take better care of herself if she expected to make it until it is warmer. In a small kitchen she put a kettle on her stove and excused herself. I stood around the small room that served as her living room and noticed several pictures in frames on the end tables. When she returned I asked her who were in the pictures. She was delighted as she described her daughter and her two grandchildren. I asked her where they lived and she became angry. "How should I know where they live? They don't call and I'm not a charity case!"

I assured her I meant no disrespect as the kettle whistle blared loudly through the apartment. She removed two cups from a cabinet above the sink. I noticed they were the only dishes in the cabinet. There was a small dish on the sink and when she opened the refrigerator it was empty except for a quart of milk and a carton of eggs. I asked if she needed me to do shopping for her. Again she became belligerent saying, "I do my own shopping! What do I look like to you?"

I mentioned there was nothing in the refrigerator and the storm outside was only going to get worse. She took a deep breath and advised she had more than enough to get by.

We sat in the living room and drank our tea. I noticed there was no television in the apartment. I asked her why. She started yelling again in a most expressive manner telling me, "Do I strike you as someone who needs to be entertained? I have a radio which is all I need to stay on top of this world we live in." I agreed with her knowing there was truly nothing on television that might give her a moment of peace. We finished the tea and I again asked if there was anything she needed. She looked at the pictures on her end tables. She said, "I'd like to know if they are ok." I left the apartment after telling her I would maintain her sidewalk. I told her it was too dangerous for her to try shoveling. In her best way she thanked me by saying, "As long as some fool doesn't fall and sue me!"

I maintained the sidewalk every few hours after clearing the snow in front of my house. It wasn't a very big deal and it didn't take much longer since I was outside anyway.

Throughout the night I noticed her light on in the living room. I could see her sitting in a chair near the window and she appeared to be talking to someone. I knew she lived alone so it was disturbing to think of her talking to herself or the photos in those frames.

This morning I went to sprinkle salt on the sidewalk and I could see the light was still on but she was gone. I figured she had gone to bed and hopefully was enjoying a good rest. A neighbor came out of the house next door and asked if I noticed the entire ruckus in the middle of the night.

I told him I had gone out to shovel around midnight but saw nothing out of the ordinary. He told me "an ambulance came and carted the old lady away." I asked him, "You mean Moxie?" He laughed saying, "Is that what she told you her name was, she was a hoot." I asked him what her real name was and he could not remember. I asked him why he doubted she told me her real name and he said, "Because Moxie died ten years ago." "Who was Moxie?" I asked confused.

"That was her daughter."

"But what about her grandchildren, I saw pictures in frames?"

"She doesn't have any grandchildren. Moxie was her only child."

I made inquiries at the local hospitals and because I'm not a blood relative no one would tell me where she was taken. I contacted the ambulances and the same thing. And now she's gone."

The waitress reached over and patted his hand. She poured him another cup of coffee asking why he kept checking his phone.

"I'm waiting for Moxie to call me. I gave her my number."

SOPHIE
11PM

At eleven o'clock that evening, I picked up my youngest son who lay sleeping beside my daughter and carried him to his own bed. He woke up crying. My wife tried reasoning with him, to no avail. I suggested she should try to get some sleep and I'd try talking to him. He wouldn't listen until I told him, "no matter what, he is never alone." He stopped crying and his little voice asked, "What?" I explained that, even though everyone was asleep, he could talk to me if he wanted. He said he did not want to talk to me.

Cast out of his room, I went into the bathroom. When I came out, I heard him talking to someone. I stood in the hallway listening, not wanting to interrupt his conversation. He was explaining to someone that we had four beds in this house and whoever it was could pick any bed he or she wanted to sleep in. He mentioned that his friends, Crystal, Steven and Michael could all come over to see him whenever they wanted to play. He started a chant that lasted quite a while saying over and over again – "Tomorrow, I go to school, Tomorrow I go to school." Then he said in a curious voice, "Do you go to school? Tomorrow I go to school."

There was a period of silence and I felt this concert of innocence had ended. I stood outside his door leaning against a wall, listening closely to every sound: hearing him take a drink from his cup of juice, adjusting his covers. Just as I was ready to walk away, he started talking again. "My sister's in her bed. My brother's in his bed. Mommy is in her bed and Daddy's……" There was a brief moment of hesitation then the ruffling of covering being undone. Hearing his little feet on the carpet, I jumped to the side, hoping I would not scare him. He walked past me and looked in the bed where my wife lay sleeping. Eyes adjusting to the darkness quickly, he ran past me and back to his bed. I heard him say, ".....and Daddy sleeps standing up." I almost burst with laughter, but managed to hold it in.

Soon, I heard the rhythmic breathing of sleep. He had finished his survey of the area making certain everyone was home. I walked downstairs to check the doors and windows, my nightly ritual. Looking out the front window, I noticed the elderly woman who lived next door standing on her porch, holding a coat over her arm, and watching intently up the block. I decided I should check to see if she was all right. I walked outside and approached her slowly. Seeing me, she immediately began explaining how her husband had been dragged away and how the owner of the house had robbed him. She was determined to walk up the block and look for her husband. She said something in German and my face must have dictated a lack of understanding. She said, "You don't believe me?" I tried to comfort her by saying "Everything is going to be okay if she would go inside and wait." "NO, NO!" she said. "He needs me. He doesn't have his coat and its cold!" I assured her he would be all right.

She said she called the police and they were looking for him, too. Her upstairs neighbor came to the window saying, "Is she out again?" Joining us on the porch, the neighbor nodded in my direction and said, "Sophie, its okay. You should go inside now."

She reiterated her story about her husband to the neighbor, suggesting he call the police and wait until they came. Watching Sophie walk ever so slowly into her house, I waved to the neighbor feeling sad.

Sophie's husband had been taken away in an ambulance almost two years ago; he died at the hospital. In her aged wisdom, the innocence of waiting for someone to come home had mixed reality with something perhaps only little voices, speaking in the darkness, could understand. I went back into my house, locked the door and watched through a side window.

As the neighbor slowly turned on the lights in Sophie's apartment, I could see through the shades that he was trying, without success, to reason with her. I could not hear, but I knew she had plans for tomorrow that are promised each day.

The young can feel it. It keeps them awake with vibrant joy. The elderly feel it and it and it keeps them awake with misunderstood woe. I stood motionless in the darkness for quite a while before checking all the rooms one last time; knowing time is something relevant that we call take for granted, day in and day out. I listened to the sounds only silence can make more profound. Softly I said out loud, "Good night, Sophie."

THE JAZZ KING MIDNIGHT

At midnight the streets take on a glow that welcome shadows through the trees. Walking after midnight down any main street in America takes on a shared silence that echoes from the day before.

Bobbie Rugio was trying to come to grips with the loss of his father. His memories were scattered belonging to another time and place. As he walked along Metropolitan Avenue he felt the presence of his father in every step. He remembered going to Eddie's Sweet Shop and his father announcing to the entire place – "This round is on me!" Bobbie Rugio never again knew anyone who bought everyone ice cream on a hot summer night.

Staring up at the marquee of the Cinemart Movie Theater he remembered going to see "To Kill a Mockingbird" with his entire family. He remembered the part when the reverend says "stand up, your father's passing." It was moment that made him proud of his father as if he were Atticus Finch himself. When they left the theater his Dad proclaimed a "second round at Eddie's" and they ran as a soft rain fell. He remembered looking down the avenue at the streetlamps with the rain coming down making them look as if they were shimmering off and on like in a dream.

Robbie Rugio called his father The Jazz King. It was in honor of his knowledge of all things related to jazz music. It was also because his father had a special quality for being in the right places at the right time. He sat next to many of the jazz greats in his time after they finished a set at the Village Vanguard, Birdland, The Blue Note and the Five Spot in Manhattan.

When his father came home at night he told the best stories until Bobbie's head was spinning with music. When the rest of the world was hearing about books being banned and the loss of morality in America, The Jazz King gave him his paperback copies of Henry Miller's Tropic of Capricorn and Tropic of Cancer. He told him, "There's no worse morality than having puritanism shoved down your throat."

Through the years after Bobbie set out on his own he always tried to stay in touch with his family.

Even when he knew he was testing the waters outside of any expectations they may have had for him. He knew his father would support him and never judge his choices. With the Jazz King's passing came a new realization about his own mortality. He walked on the streets where he grew up and tried to see if anything from his past could have changed anything he chose to do.

Not one street corner or any memory about shard ice cream or movie choices made a difference. He could hear his father's voice in his head saying, "If you get to a place and have no need to look back, you will be happy. If you get to a place and feel a need to think about yesterday, you will be happy. It's the getting to anywhere that matters most."

It had been years since Bobbie Rugio had been in his hometown. He thought about things in a way that his father listened to music. Life for him was one song after another in to the night.

The memories he knew would God willing always be there. Unlike the thief that stole his father's memories without any remorse. Once when he was just a boy his father told him something that at the time made them both laugh all the way home.

They were out walking and The Jazz King said, "You see this road? It's always going to go that way and this way in a straight line. The people on both sides are going to come and go, the buildings may change but the road stays the same."

Standing in the middle of Metropolitan Avenue as a soft rain began to fall he looked up in the sky and knew The Jazz King was watching.

NORMAL
2AM

You are trying to tell me this is normal? What kind of normal are you expecting me to accept? Your normal is not my normal. If everyone's definition of normal was the same just imagine how abnormal that would be? If I considered your normal, would you consider mine?

The conversation was so out of the ordinary I had to pay closer attention to the man expressing himself outside the corner delicatessen. He was carrying on in such a way as to make this incident surreal. His demeanor was such that several neighbors discussed calling the police.

It was not normal to see someone talking in a way that made everyone around uncomfortable. The man continued his ranting related to living life in the modern world.

"Now then," he said, "you expect me to abide by your standards without realizing I have standards too. I can no longer tolerate the same things you say I have to. In the same way, you can only listen to me for shorter and shorter periods of time before finding what I say annoying. Who's to bless and who's to blame? That's the only question we should be discussing right now. If you embrace your values then I should embrace them too? And yet, here I am challenging you to accept me as I am but you find that cumbersome. What kind of value oriented society asks people to accept things one way without considering the other way?"

A man walking his dog came upon the scene noticing several people had their phones out recording this most odd moment. He listened to the man continuing his rant.

"All I am saying is if everyone wants to give peace a chance, how come we are always hearing about war? Who gets to decide what peace means and when we go to war? I'm not for war and still I know if I continue to talk like this I'll be disturbing the peace. Whose peace am I disturbing? You can't have it both ways?"

The man with the dog sensing the growing impatience of the assembled crowd approached him slowly. Standing with his dog at his side he asked the confused man if he needed something he could not find.

"What kind of something could make me feel better?" The man responded looking at his dog and backing away.

"Do you think I am afraid of your dog?"

The man pulled back on the dogs leash saying, "How do you know my dog is not afraid of you?"

"Why would he be afraid of me? I did nothing to bother him. Listen I don't want to scare your dog."

"Then tell him, not me?"

"You want me to tell your dog I don't mean any harm?"

"It's a start. Otherwise he's going to feel threatened."

"I'm not trying to scare you," he said leaning down to pet the dog.

The man's dog sat and allowed the man to pet his head.

The dog looked at the confused soul in the eyes and licked his face.

"Hey your dog licked me face! No one touches my face."

"How did it feel?"

"It felt strangely sincere. How did you train your dog to be sincere?"

"It comes natural to him. If you're nice to him he will be nice to you."

"How come humans can't do that?"

"I have been trying to understand that my whole life."

In the distance the sound of a siren could be heard coming down the avenue. The man with the dog asked the confused man if he wanted to help him walk his dog.

"You mean like I can hold his leash and follow him?"

"If that's how you want to do it, fine."

He handed the man the dogs leash and they walked down a side street away from the crowd. When the police arrived several people tried to explain why they were called.

The policeman asked where the man went. They pointed down the street where they had gone. The street was empty except for a woman standing on her stoop talking on her phone.

The police approached her asking if she saw anything out of the ordinary. She said yes, there were a bunch of people harassing a man trying to save the world.

ANYWHERE
3AM

Artie was not happy about what he needed to do. It was his wedding anniversary and his wife expected him to plan a celebration. He was sitting near the overpass of the trestle at the end of Cooper Avenue talking to a friend.

"That we have to go anywhere after all this time is worrisome. Isn't there a time when being together is enough? I realize it's a special occasion and most people believe we should celebrate being together this long. I hate showing off. That we lasted as long as we have is something of a small miracle. I know a thing or two about miracles. I have three children."

"But no here we are on this day and its necessary we go out anywhere to toast to our success. What's worse is she left it to me to choose where anywhere might be. I know what you are thinking – who worries about such things?"

"I am cursed with overthinking everything. So where does one take someone who means everything to him? Not just anywhere will do. I could make reservations at a restaurant in Manhattan."

"Some place fancy where they expect the customers to dress up. I could go maybe to one of those real swanky places with waiters who are called maitre d's wearing tuxedos and speaking in fake accents. I could take her someplace where the wine list cost more than everything on the menu in a local place here."

"I want to take her anywhere that makes her know how I feel. We have been together too long for her to believe what I say. It's gotten to the point there's more time in our past than possible in our future."

"At weddings when they play the Anniversary Waltz we are most likely to be the last couple standing. We don't pay it much mind when dancing because after looking around and seeing the youthful faces of newlyweds and younger couples it's a far gone conclusion how it will turn out."

"We never discuss our comments when the deejay holds a microphone in front of our faces asking if we have any advice for the newlyweds. She gets a look of happiness on her face and says something like "compromise." I always try to be more realistic by saying something like "certain things last.""

"It always makes for a moment of clarity which I don't provide. But where does anyone take the person who means everything to him? I could go out on the limb and make a sob story like "I didn't feel well all day." She would be understanding and immediately try to make me feel better. I would hate myself for being a coward. I would despise myself for not knowing where to take her. If only anywhere had a name?"

"After so many years there's no use trying to put something in a card or buying a piece of jewelry she always wanted. Those things are for the newlywed couples. Those things are for the old fools who think themselves in need of a much younger wife. The kind of wife he will always have to keep content or she will leave him."

"The couples who stayed the course, we suffer the slings and arrows of time. It erases things we took for granted for so long. And yet how can I explain my miracle? How is it she has defied aging? How is it she still finds me amusing?"

"Go anywhere else on the planet and you will not find anyone like her. The ways I tested her through the years deserves my immediate incarceration. At best I should be under house arrest."

"Maybe that's what I will tell her – I can't leave the house because I am being monitored by the police. That won't work; it never did in the past. We will settle for some place less than what she deserves. Some place cozy with a corner table in the back. She'll order a glass of wine and the lights will twinkle in her eyes like the way they do when she looks at me after I made one of my stupid remarks."

"The worst that could happen is we meet somebody we know. Telling them we are celebrating our special occasion in the same place they decided to drop in to for a meal will make me feel great. I will have to look at the couple in the humble way I can knowing what they are thinking – Couldn't you have taken her anywhere else?"

"Thankfully it only happens once a year. Sooner or later we'll be too old to give it a second thought. The problem is it will always matter. Anywhere we go people will say things like – "I can't believe they are still together," or "She stayed married to him?"

"When I think of where someone with lots of success could have taken her it makes me nuts. How different would she look in the arms of some rich guy? I hope she knows she may have gone to nicer places to eat but the rich guy would never see what I do. As a matter of fact I should take her anywhere that is certain to have rich guys sitting at other tables."

"I want to show her off. I want to compare my trophy next to theirs. I want to order something so expensive we miss a mortgage payment. I want the Chef in some fancy place to come to our table and hear my wife tell him one of her recipes. I want to see his eyes bugging out of his head when he realizes how amazing it sounds to use ingredients his brain never comprehended."

"I want to go anywhere that has music playing. Not the overhead sound systems that echo through cheap ceiling tiles. Anywhere that has live music where the band plays requests. Anywhere has a name. It's called home.'

Sitting and looking down along Cooper Avenue he noticed his friend was smiling. "What's so damn amusing?" he asked. His friend shrugged saying, "You already know where you want to go. Why are you second guessing yourself?"

"If I take her to Woodhaven House, she's going to think I didn't give the dinner enough thought. She knows it's my favorite place to go. I like the atmosphere and once I heard a song from the jukebox I never heard anywhere else."

"She likes it when you hear music you like. It reminds of her of when you both were young. The way you came home after buying a new album all excited saying, "Wait till you hear this? Like the time you told me you brought home a new Van Morrison album and you both danced till dawn."

FEEDERS
4AM

Jasper Jones was a feeder. He did not know he had this distinction when growing up. As the years passed he spent most of his time sitting in the library where feeders were everywhere. The writer Sherwood Anderson said feeders were storytellers. Mr. Anderson thought anyone who told stories were feeding the world in a way that made them nurture the spirit of the human heart and soul.

Jasper Jones took his feeding seriously. He read anything he could get his hands on growing up. When he visited bookstores with his parents growing up he noticed how many people like himself enjoyed reading. As he grew older and bookstores became less available, he visited the library more and more.

Taking the same chair at the back of the library he would spend his days reading the newspapers that the library received as a courtesy from the different publishers. He noticed the papers became less and less about the news and more and more about the opinions of the writers and editors.

Jasper Jones told anyone willing to listen, "news is not open to interpretation." He could not put his finger on when exactly this new form of journalism came in to being. He felt it was a sin to report things with a political slant. He felt it was a travesty for writers to tell what happened without telling the truth.

Jasper Jones once considered himself a writer. He started a local paper he called "The Here Now News." In his paper which he wrote every story about things that happened around his community took on an air of reality. He likened his reporting style to old newspaper stories his father made him read out loud when he was a young boy.

The few people who subscribed to his paper canceled their subscriptions after the first month of publication. They said, "all of these stories are written by the same person and we can't believe what they say." He was disappointed by his failure to bring the truth to his neighborhood. He knew what he wrote was real but realized people enjoy sensationalism more than anything else.

His second attempt at "The Here Now News" took a page from the magazine's he saw in supermarkets which told tales so far from the truth they were almost laughable. His first headline story in the newly revised Here Now News read as follows:

Serpent Wipes Out Entire Neighborhood

As the rain fell heavily houses were swept off their foundations and swallowed by a giant serpent. A manhole cover on Cooper Avenue left open after the storm showed the remnants of where the 50 foot snake escaped to wreak havoc through the neighborhood. Mrs. Haley Summersall witnessed the event and shared her story.

She said, "Well first thing I noticed is how fast the rain was coming down. The sewer system could never handle such a downpour. Next thing the manhole covers started lifting out of the ground and floating like Frisbees down the street. Then I heard a loud rumble come out of the ground and there it was - the serpent everyone knew was down there but never saw. It was just horrible! It leaped out of the ground at a passing car and swallowed it in one huge gulp.

Then it attacked my neighbor's home leaving nothing but bursting pipes spraying water everywhere.

Several people have reported seeing the serpent headed in to the cemetery on Myrtle Avenue. The National Guard has been summoned by the Mayor who was last seen on a horse and carriage trying to survey the damage.

The circulation of the Here Now News went through the roof. Jasper Jones had to hire a staff of people to work day and night printing the paper to meet demands. Realizing his readers enjoyed stories that depicted the worst case scenario possible he published more and more outlandish things.

Woman Stampedes Avenue

A large woman of 72 feet in height attacked the local mall today. She demanded to meet with the town officials who when summoned were last seen in a VW Microbus heading north on the New York State Thruway. In an effort to make her point, the large female stampeded through the mall leaving nothing of value in its path.

While chasing the town officials who had been hiding in a burnt out basement the suspect marched up 80th street and entered the park.

From her tower like vantage point she saw the officials and started running as fast as a 72 foot woman in high heels could run. The heels were the brainstorm of fashion designer Enrico Deplam who last year made the shoes for Daryl Hannah and Natalie Portman in their movie version of Beasts of Burden. On the red carpet at this year's Oscars Enrico promised something big.

We can only imagine if this is what he meant but the fashion world is following this story closely.

The 72 foot beauty was last seen in pursuit of the town's officials who realizing they were being followed changed cars with a visiting couple from Peoria Illinois. The couple was trampled to death by the woman who recognizing she had been duped vowed to catch the officials if it was the last thing she ever did.

Jasper Jones needed to hire more writers. He asked the local schools if they had children who were aspiring authors. Once certain he had the right staff assembled he set out to triple his circulation. In the first month after hiring the new writers he needed to hire a distribution manager. The home delivery of the Here Now News enabled Jasper Jones to purchase buildings along the backstreets of Otto Road.

There he began construction of the largest insane asylum this side of the Mississippi River. He sent out flyers along with his newspapers advertising the Here Now News Institution for the Gullible and Incurable. By summer he had a waiting list for rooms that forced residents in Glendale to consider him the biggest investor in the community since its birth back in the 19th century.

Jasper needed to add more buildings with more floors as the years passed. The United States census bureau realizing there were now more people in institutions in one community than anywhere else in the world named Glendale the Institutional Capital of America.

With most residents safely in the Otto Road Correctional Facility Jasper Jones was the richest real estate magnate in the world. He sold the abandoned homes people left when they flocked to his institutions at rock bottom prices to people who passed a simple handwritten test. There was one question on the test. This was the question:

What is wrong with you people?

Anyone willing to answer the question honestly was given a new place to live. Those who took offense to the question were invited to take up residence in the institutions. It was a plan so well developed the U.S. Government started copying the plan around the nation.

It is believed by the year 2050 most people in America will live in institutions. The homes they leave behind will be redeveloped and sold to any and all people who can honestly answer the question - What is wrong with you people?

In a very rare interview with the press Jasper Jones when asked what the right answer to the question might be, he responded with a one word answer. Everything.

THE B&B
5AM

No one when asked could remember how the position came in to existence. Many believe it happened after so many changes occurred around the world it became necessary to assign someone to keep track of things. While researching the first place that displayed a job notice for the position was found tacked to a bulletin board at the local grocery store:

New Job Notice - The position of town gossip has been hereby recognized as a viable and necessary job by the state commission.

The town B and B (busy body) will have the following credentials and traits:

(1) Must be highly agitated
(2) Able to speak coherently while demeaning everything and everyone
(3) Has no close ties to any local religious organizations
(4) Considers rudeness an attribute
(5) Can talk trash in several languages
(6) Has no affiliation with any political party
(7) Hates everyone and everything equally
(8) Enjoys watching hours of reality television
(9) Believes OJ Simpson was innocent
(10) Drinks tea and believes England should take back America

The thought of finding anyone who would match the required credentials became a bone of contention for local residents. Several men and women came forward but none seemed to have the proper feel. Despite many candidates being turned down for months it was only by coincidence the right person showed up after hollering at a store owner for not having his groceries in alphabetical order on the shelves.

So many townspeople watched the YouTube video of her demanding food be properly displayed to her liking that an immediate interview was set up by the community board. The very concept of her showing up at all at the offices of the chamber of commerce was enough to convince everyone they had found the best person for the job.

Illouise Momsburben was named the Glendale B&B in a ceremony that had thousands of people cheering in recognition of her rare talents to despise everyone and everything about Glendale. When asked the deciding question on the local news she answered so quickly it made people applaud her as the most deplorable yet desirable person for the job. "Why do you live here?" She said, "It's the same as anywhere else and all the people are the same!"

In her first week as the Busy Body Specialist, Illouise managed to insult anyone who owned a car. "You people think you own the roads! All hours of the day and night coming and going without regard for the sleeping! You can't park without taking up spaces that don't belong to you!"

The community was joyous in celebrating her rude behavior in the face of things bothering everyone that they commissioned a bronze statue of Illouise placed at the center of Glendale. Fights broke out when individuals could not agree on where the middle of Glendale existed.

Her comments went viral when she took on the environmentalist by saying "If my garbage is so damn important why don't you pick it up in limousines instead of these trucks with breaks that make more noise than jets landing at an airport!" Her attitude was exactly what the community needed. When visiting local stores she was quick to give them lip too. "You don't even know who your customers are! You should know them by name and offer to stock whatever they need to make them happy!"

The town council needed to hire more people to keep track of the phone calls coming in every day demanding she be fired. Her presence raised the bar in how others treated one another with common courtesy. No one wanted to experience the wrath of the B&B. The local police noticed their crime levels diminished because the criminals themselves were too afraid to step out of line. She took the job so seriously the state commissioned she receive a special award.

The Rude Award was bestowed upon her in a ceremony held at City Hall. In a speech thanking the state for recognition she lambasted the Mayor for being a baboon and the governor for being a mobster.

It started a whirlwind of recognition that went nationwide. In a nationwide vote Illouise Momsburden was named the best B&B in America.

When the next election rolled around she was hands down to be named a candidate for a political party. In a speech she noted, "Being a member of either party would make me privy to things I don't care about. If I am to run for office I want to do it from my own platform!"

As the first presidential candidate for the B&B party she caused widespread panic beyond the nations wildest imaginations. No one would run against her in her own party so the first time she had debates was with candidates from the Democratic and Republican parties two months before the national election.

In the first debate she called the Democratic nominee Judas. She said "you'd take money to crucify your own mother!" She told the Republican candidate "you tell more lies than members of NASA!" After the debate she received death threats. She hired the Hells Angels to protect her after they volunteered to take her wherever she wanted to go. She called them "a bunch of red neck hippies!" But she agreed they had her best interest at heart. Without any campaign committee and at no cost to the tax payers of America she won the election in a landslide victory.

Her first order of business once in the White House was to demand the congress be dismantled, the House of Representatives excused from their duties and all military personnel be put on a permanent state of alert.

In her first public announcement in front of the entire country she said, **Wake up or Get Out**.

This became the B&B slogan for the remainder of the 21st century. There were no wars and very little condemnation of America during the remaining years of the century. No other party except the B&B served the country again. When leaving office after her 12 years as President Illouise Momsburden said, "I'd stay longer but you people scare me!"

THEATRE 6AM

Recently unbeknownst to most people in the neighborhood a local theater company dispensed with the staging of a disturbing play. The play was set in a futuristic society where everyone guarded their homes with guns and weapons of mass destruction. The paranoid nature of the residents was so intense the audience left the theater running to their cars. The theatre in response to the overwhelming demand for tickets started a lottery called "The IAON Fund."

The IAON fund named after the title of the play "It's All Over Now" has thus far collected upwards of a half million dollars in contributions. The money from the fund will be used to construct a new theatre located somewhere here in the community. Local businessmen have been asked to provide ideas for the new theatre.

Another lottery was started to collect suggestions for naming the theatre. Thus far the leading names are - Theatre of the Absurd and Paranoid Theatre. Both names are being bandied about with another lottery being suggested to commission logos for each. It is believed the citizens will be able to vote on which name and logo best represents the community come election time.

Placing this item on the election ballot has caused several members of the community board to resign in disgust. Notwithstanding the many people who feel they have what it takes to act on stage have caused wars to break out everywhere. The local police have begun labeling areas of the community with new names.

The Shakespeare area of the community the men and women have taken to wearing clothes straight out of Ancient Rome and Victorian England. These people are considered extremely dangerous and are often seen carrying swords and large spears.

In the Tennessee Williams area the habitual nature of the people has resorted to public drunkenness complete with male rowdiness and female women of ill repute.

In the Arthur Miller area individuals wishing to sell everything and anything have clogged streets and caused near riots with 24 hour long flea markets.

A most disturbing section of the community known by the police as the Sam Shepard's has people running around yelling obscenities and dragging wild horses and mules while threatening to kill family members who are not in keeping with the codes of the old West.

To make matters worse the Eugene O' Neil society for theatrical presentation has sued the community for making a mockery of theatre as an art form. In response to this most disturbing classification the Manhattan District Court has demanded the town of Glendale and its residents be placed under martial law. The National Guard has been brought in to the town to maintain order.

In a speech at the local board meeting Ismeal Humbergartin of the community had this to say, "This is a to be or not to be moment in our community. Who amongst us dare question the value of theatre in a place void of so many similar characters? Not one amongst us can rationalize such worth without condemning the travesty of so many differences.

Our diversity has become our curse. The duress will be our undoing. Already the absurdity of our true nature has caused us to fight block against block and neighbor versus neighbor. We are the very meaning of theatre with our comedic and tragic ignorance on display in full costume dress."

The local Facebook page was closed due to comments considered by the Internet to be too graphic and obscene for public consumption. To calm the community separation a bipartisan theatre company from Stockbridge Massachusetts will perform Thornton Wilder's Our Town nonstop over the upcoming weekend at the Forest Park band shell. The National Guard will be patrolling the area along with the local police to ward off any potential terrorist attacks.

Local residents are asked to arrive early for limited seating. A procession to make the final scene of the play more realistic for it takes place in a cemetery will commence on the hour down Myrtle Avenue, Metropolitan Avenue and Cooper Avenue in to the entrances of cemeteries in the community. A candle light vigil will be held with a fireworks display after midnight.

The first annual Welcome to the Absurd parade will take place on the first Sunday of next month. All those wishing to march are asked to leave their masks at home.

ANGELS
7:00 AM

She doesn't like to talk about it. It's nobody's business anyway. She used to go to every game with her father. He had season tickets from his job. She saw them at their best and when losing. Not that they were ever losers in our eyes, but if you must know, they didn't win much in the late 1960s.

June 8th, 1969 was the last game she had anything to talk about in a big way. That's the day the Yankees retired Mickey Mantle's number. She grew up with her Dad's love of the game. They went to every game together. When the season started her father would show up at school telling the teachers there was a family emergency and they would be off to the big ball park laughing.

People say she stopped talking about baseball like only she could for years when they tore the old stadium down. She was there to watch them knock the old park down. She had no interest in the big shiny new stadium with the same name. The last thing she said about it was that it was sacrilegious. Can you imagine what she saw sitting in that stadium every day from the age of 5 years old in the 1950s straight on through to the last day when they tore it down? She once told me Derek Jeter was blessed by the angels in the outfield.

I don't like to talk about it much either if you want to know the truth. I had the biggest crush on her and she only had eyes for Mickey Mantle. He was her hero. Her Dad had raised her like no other girl you ever met. She knew more about Baseball history than anyone I ever met.

But it wasn't just about the Yankees, it was more than that -- something about a love of the game which made her the most interesting girl you ever wanted to know.

When we would meet up going to High School on the Myrtle Avenue bus she would be reading the newspaper. Not to read about the game the Yankees won or lost the day before, but studying the stats to see who was pitching and what to expect from the next game. I got to go with her a few times. The company her Dad worked for let him have the box seats near the Yankee dugout and man let me tell you, there's nothing like sitting so close to the field you can breathe in the smell of the grass.

A few times her Dad when he was starting to get sick would get an extra ticket and I would go as the fourth person in the box with her and her mother. I don't think her Mom loved the game as much as she and her Dad. There was nothing like eating a hot dog with your eyes peeled toward home plate sensing at any second you could be taking a bite and a line drive might sail right at you.

After every game we would go through this little gate that would swing open allowing the fans to walk out on to the field and through the outfield fences on to the street. Let me tell you I never walked so slow my whole life as when I got to do that. Leaning down and picking up a handful of infield dirt or grabbing blades of grass right where Mickey Mantle stood during the games. I went only a half a dozen times through the years with her in those days. After high school she went to school upstate and I got letters from her every once in a while telling me about how she would take the train and meet her Dad in the city before going to games.

That was in the late 1960s when the Yankees weren't doing too good. It didn't stop us from cheering them on. I was with her that day in June 1969. She called me the day before and asked me to meet her at her house off 80th street. Standing on 78th avenue she came out of her house carrying a big bag. When she told me what she planned to do I was almost too afraid to go through with it. I asked her if she told her mother what we were going to do. She told me not to worry about it.

We walked over the 80th street bridge and on to a staircase that went down near the railroad tracks. She opened the bag and we stuffed our pockets as full as we could. She had told me to wear a jacket and we both stuffed those pockets full too. What was left in little bags she stuffed in to the sleeves of her jacket and carried it.

We had to take the train to the stadium. We watched Mickey Mantle talk about understanding what Lou Gehrig meant about being the luckiest man alive when he retired. We watched Joe DiMaggio present Mickey with a plaque that would sit right next to his in the outfield. Through it all she cried and it was the first time I truly felt love for someone in a way I can't talk about now.

When the game was over we exited on to the field and slowly made our way to the outfield fences. Every step of the way we let her father's ashes out of our pockets. At the outfield fence she removed what was left in the bags stuffed in her sleeves and she sprinkled them on the warning track. A few times we got scared someone was going to make us stop, but everyone was sort of in their own little dazed world.

She continued going to games alone for years after that. She couldn't afford the box seats her Dad once had so she sat in the bleachers where the bums screamed out the names of each player until they were acknowledged. She told me in letters those fans made her feel the spirit of her Dad lifting off the field. When her mom passed she took a handful of her ashes and poured them over the outfield wall on to the warning track. It was the best she could do because no one was allowed on the field anymore.

She wrote in a letter how it felt to sit in the stands knowing her parents were together forever. She said it made her smile whenever Mariano Rivera would go in to a game with the crowd yelling as his theme song, Enter Sandman by Metallica filled the stadium. A few times I saw her on television when Rivera left the bullpen. She was the old lady with her arms outstretched, her head raised to the sky with her eyes closed.

When they knocked down the real Yankee Stadium she vowed to never again watch a game. She sent me a letter that had a single sentence. She wrote, "Angels don't move across the street."

Made in the USA
Middletown, DE
10 June 2017